OCT 25			

SO-BAQ-628

THE
WITCH KING

THE
WITCH KING

Maeve Henry

ORCHARD BOOKS

A division of Franklin Watts, Inc.

New York & London

For my mother

ORCHARD BOOKS
387 Park Avenue South
New York, New York 10016

ORCHARD BOOKS CANADA
20 Torbay Road
Markham, Ontario 23P 1G6

Orchard Books is a division of Franklin Watts, Inc.

MANUFACTURED IN THE UNITED STATES OF AMERICA

Book design by Tere LoPrete

10 9 8 7 6 5 4 3 2 1

The text of this book is set in Garamond No. 3

Library of Congress Cataloging-in-Publication Data

Henry, Maeve.
    The witch king.

    Summary: Fifteen-year-old Robert, an ordinary
village boy, travels to the capital city where, with
the aid of magic, he conquers palace intrigue and
discovers his destiny as the legendary Witch King.
    [1. Magic—Fiction. 2. Wizards—Fiction] I. Title
PZ7.H39397Ei 1988   [Fic]   87-20370
ISBN 0-531-05738-0
ISBN 0-531-08338-1 (lib. bdg.)

PROLOGUE

———— ◆•◆ ————

When the winter wind is howling off the sea, stories are told by the fire in the fishing villages along the northern coast. They tell of a kingdom to the south, and of a City and its kings, long ago. As night presses at the window and the fire burns low, one story especially chills the heart of those who hear it. It is the story of how Leo became king.

When Leo arrived in the City the leaves were turning gold. He never told anyone where he came from, so no one ever knew. Some people liked him, and some did not: he had a handsome face but it was cold and cunning.

After one adventure and another he fell in with a nobleman who took him to the king's palace to meet the king's sister. Princess Judith was beautiful and gentle and as she was old enough to marry, all the great lords of the City had come asking for her hand. Judith cared for none of them and laughed when they were mentioned. But when she saw Leo, she fell in love. His handsome face and quick wits won her heart at once.

To the anger of all the lords, King Mark her brother was willing to let her have her choice. And indeed for a while all went well. King Mark gave Leo lands and money, and Leo served him faithfully. Soon Leo was the commander of the army, and the greatest lord in the land, and if Judith was ever sorry for her choice, she hid it from her brother. Leo's first son was born, and then another, and since King Mark had no children of his own, he made the elder boy his heir. And still Leo had not achieved what he came for. It was not enough to see his son inherit a kingdom. He wanted the crown himself.

Rumors of Leo's intention reached King Mark, who grew cold and fearful. He began to look for a way to rid himself of the stranger, but before he could act, Leo struck. He led his army into the palace by night, killed King Mark with his own sword and forced the panic-stricken lords to crown him. Then he returned in triumph to his wife and children. He found Judith in the nursery, rocking her two dead sons in her arms, laughing and singing to them. Her clothes and the floor around her were soaked in blood. For as the soldiers burst into the palace, King Mark had had time to give his servants one last command.

So King Mark had his revenge on Leo; but it was Judith who suffered most of all. She never recovered her senses after that night, but was mad for the rest of her life. As for Leo, he took another wife and had more sons. He ruled the kingdom so harshly that no one dared speak of how he came by it. But because he was afraid that someone else might use the army just as he had, he devised a new and secret way to guard himself and the City from all enemies.

No one who told his story in the north could say what that way might be.

ONE

Robert Harding stuck his head out of the bedclothes and found that the sunlight from the tiny window opposite was even warmer than blankets. He stretched like a cat and yawned. His father and older brothers had got up before the sun and gone out to sea in their boat. When the sun rose it had found them already catching fish. Robert just groaned at the thought of it and nestled back in his blankets, singing softly to himself a song about a king in a faraway land. From the kitchen below came the sound of pots banging on the stove. It was time to get up.

"Robert!" his mother shouted from the foot of the dark little staircase. "Ro-bert!"

He scrambled out of bed at once, hungry for breakfast, and put on his shirt and some pants. But before he went down he slid past the bed to the window and looked out at the sea. As he stared at the glassy green waves he remembered a dream he had had in the night. Robert often had strange dreams, but this was stranger than most. It was of a picture made out of stones, a chaotic swirling of purple and black and green. The memory of it shook him. During the dream he had been terrified; even now his muscles tensed and his mind stirred uneasily. What was there to fear in a picture of stones?

His mother was standing at the table, ladling the thick porridge into a bowl. As soon as she saw Robert she smiled and shook her head, and Robert smiled back and grew calm again. He ate his porridge with relish, watching his mother as she bustled about. He was dark like her, and rather small for a boy of fifteen, while his brothers took after their father and were tall and fair.

"Haven't you finished yet?" she cried suddenly. "The school bell will be sounding in another minute!" She cut a large slice of bread and gave it to him. "You'd better eat this on the way. But don't dawdle!"

"I won't," Robert promised, as he promised every morning. He ran his finger along the inside of his porridge bowl and licked it, winked at the cat under the table and strolled out into the fine sea-fresh air.

He set off at a quick pace, with the best of intentions. But the narrow stone building up on the hill had such a grim and discouraging look as Robert approached it that he came to a halt. He was always beaten, whether he was a minute or an hour late; he might as well sit down on the grass beside the path and enjoy his piece of bread. Down below he could see the straggling line of whitewashed cottages that formed the village and the beach that swept right up to their front doors. He took a pattern of bites out of his bread and began to think about his dream.

If you want something badly enough, it will fill your thoughts when you are awake and your dreams when you

are asleep. That was how it was for Robert. He was certain
his dream concerned his heart's desire, though he could not
yet see how. The desire of Robert's heart was to find his
way to the kingdom far to the south and to the City at the
heart of it.

Stories about the City had been told in the village as long
as anyone could remember. The smallest child in the dark
classroom up on the hill knew the story of how the City had
been built, long ago before anyone lived by the sea or caught
fish for a living. A young man had come walking along a
beach, it was said, when something on the cliff above caught
his eye. When he climbed to the top he found a tree with
silver leaves, and, beside it, an ax. The young man took the
ax and cut down the tree and began to build, singing as he
worked, and because the tree was magic everything he built
turned into stone. But he built so hard and so fast that as the
City rose up the green land expanded and the sea grew
further away until in the end it was no more than a memory.

Other men and women had come to help him as he
worked, and when the work was done the young man became king and the others lived with him. The scent of the
tree's leaves and the song the young man had sung lingered
in the City like a kind of magic. It became the City of crafts-
men skilled in wood and stone, of fine musicians and famous
painters. It became the City of thinkers and adventurers,
of women who measured the stars and men who wandered
into magic lands and returned speaking strange tongues and
telling stranger tales.

Travelers from the City had often visited the lands to the
north of the kingdom in the old days. Kings had journeyed

to consult the Witch Women who lived in the little villages among the bleak hills or along the coast, for it was recognized that the City had one kind of magic, but what the Witch Women knew was better. There had been no visitor from the northern land for generations, however, and no one knew why. The Witch Women, too, had vanished from the villages long before Robert was born. The way south to the kingdom was forgotten, the few who had set out long ago to find it had never returned. Only the stories of the old days remained and were told on winter evenings. And only Robert believed the stories.

His favorite story told how the young man had saved a seed from the tree in case a time came when the City lost the scent of the leaves and the memory of the song he had sung. When that time came, the story said, a new king called the Witch King would plant the seed and renew the City. The king's name was a strange one. Robert often wondered what it meant. But he longed very much to see that story come true. He thought the City's long silence must mean the time of renewal was near. All his dreams, all his thoughts leaned to it. He was determined that one day he would set out before even the birds were up and go and seek the City.

The school bell rang for the midday break and the boys and girls ran whooping and yelling into the noon sunshine and began to descend the hill to their dinners. Robert blinked in surprise. He had not noticed the time passing and he still had not solved the puzzle of his dream. He knew only one person who might be able to tell him what it meant. He set off across the hill, over its steep sides, and down into a little empty bay next up the coast from the village.

TWO

There was no path on the other side of the hill. Robert scrambled down over the tough, cutting grass and among the dunes toward a low-roofed shack. It was made from driftwood and tarred planks, slates and flat stones, all lashed together with seaweed and old ropes, and lined with feathers, dried grass and the wool of stray sheep. This was Granny Fishbone's house. No one knew exactly who she was or how long she had lived there. The village children said the old woman was mad and ran when they saw her coming. But Robert visited her as often as he could, for Granny Fishbone knew all the stories there ever were about the City, though she grumbled about telling them.

The door of the hut faced inland, for Granny Fishbone said only a fool would build a house with its door facing the sea; that was simply inviting the sea to make itself at home. Robert knocked as loudly as he could, for the wind whistling around the hut on stormy nights had made Granny Fishbone rather deaf.

"Door's on the latch. You can come in!"

Though the day was warm, Granny Fishbone was crouching over a fire of sea-coal in the windowless dark of her hut. Robert knew his way well enough not to stumble against her cooking pot or knock his head against the bunches of plants hanging from the roof to dry.

"Oh, it's you." Granny Fishbone turned briefly from her fire. "Come for another story, I suppose." Robert slid into a stool beside her.

"Not exactly," he replied. "Granny Fishbone, I had a strange dream last night. I was standing in front of a picture made of stones. It terrified me, I don't know why. Can you tell me?"

Granny Fishbone continued to stare into the fire. Robert waited patiently. He did not know whether Granny Fishbone had guessed the strength of his passion for the City, or his hope of finding it some day, for he had never exactly told her. She was a difficult person to talk to, and a strange one to look at, almost as broad as she was high, for she put on a new layer of garments every winter and never took any off. She wore stout fisherman's boots and a battered hat with a seagull's feather in it. She smoked a pipe, and Robert knew as she took it out that he must turn his back politely while she rummaged among her skirts for her tobacco pouch. Once the pipe was filled and lit, Granny Fishbone grunted:

"Is it a picture like a sea in a storm?"

Robert opened his eyes wide.

"That's just what it was like! That's why every time I looked at the sea today I thought of it. However did you know?"

That was a question Granny Fishbone never answered. Instead she said:

"That picture in stones is a mosaic of the sea on a wall of the king's palace in the City."

Robert nodded and hugged his knees in satisfaction.

"I knew it had to be in the City," he said. "Did the first king put it there to remind him of the City's beginning?"

Granny Fishbone shook her head.

"It's not so old as that. It was made when the prophesies of the Witch King were written. It is no simple piece of workmanship. It has a special power of its own that will come into force when the Witch King has need of it."

"Tell me again about the Witch King," said Robert.

Granny Fishbone sat back in her chair and began in a slow, rather solemn voice:

"The Witch King shall come from the sea and return to the sea. He shall save the City yet destroy it. He is the bearer of the seed, planting the Tree for the City."

"I know about planting the Tree," said Robert, "but what does the rest of it mean? And why is he called the Witch King?"

"He is called the Witch King because he will have the blood of the Witch Women in his veins," Granny Fishbone replied. "You will understand the rest when the time comes."

"You mean I am going to see the story come true?"

Granny Fishbone fingered her tobacco pouch a moment, then her eyes peered at Robert's through the folds of puffy skin.

"You will see it. There are frightening times ahead of you, Robert Harding. I cannot be certain of the dangers you will face, but I can tell you this. What you saw in your dream belongs to the future. You dreamed that dream because the City is seeking you. I think it is time you set out."

As she spoke Robert was filled with a mixture of terror and joy. He got to his feet, half dazed, and stared at the old woman hunched in her chair by the fire.

"How do you know these things?" he whispered.

"You'd do better to ask what your parents will say when they find out you're bound for the City," Granny Fishbone snapped.

"But they'll never let me go," said Robert.

Granny Fishbone snorted. "Are they planning to cut off your legs?"

"But how can I go without asking?" Robert flapped his arms against his sides, driven almost to distraction. "How can I possibly go unless they agree?"

"I can't make it easy for you," Granny Fishbone said. "But stay here, Robert, and what will you become? Simply the fool the village already thinks you."

She looked straight at him, and Robert was astonished to see how her eyes burned.

"Go to the City, Robert," she said fiercely. "Do what is required there and come back to the village. I tell the stories, but no one heeds them. Come back and tell them the stories are true."

Robert stared at her. Suddenly he guessed who she was.

"You're a Witch Woman, aren't you?" he said in a whisper. "Why don't you tell the villagers who you are?"

Granny Fishbone looked down at the fire.

"When the villagers stopped believing in the City, they stopped believing in us too."

Then she got up and crossed the hut to a large black chest that stood against the wall. She rummaged in it for a while, then she brought out a small package, neatly knotted in a red handkerchief.

"Here, Robert," she said. "This is for you."

Surprised, Robert took it. As he untied the handkerchief something bright fell into his lap. It was a little fish about two inches long, beautifully worked in silver, hanging by its flexible tail from a silver chain. Robert gazed at it in astonishment. He had seen nothing like it in his life.

"It came from the City," Granny Fishbone said. "Now you must take it back."

"But what is it for?" asked Robert.

"You'll learn that when you need to know it," Granny Fishbone retorted. "Stop staring at it, donkey, and put it on. You'll lose it otherwise." Robert slipped the chain over his head and hid the fish under his shirt as Granny Fishbone continued.

"We're northeast of the kingdom here, so you need to follow a track that will take you south and west. Your feet will know when they reach the kingdom. Once you get there, you'll be met."

"How will my feet know? And who will meet me?" Robert demanded, his eyes sparkling with excitement.

"The sooner you set off, the sooner you'll find out," said Granny Fishbone.

"In that case," said Robert, taking a deep breath, "I'll go tomorrow."

THREE

There was no sound in the lamplit kitchen except for the noise of the knives scraping against plates and the kettle beginning to sing. Robert pushed his supper away half finished. He was worrying so hard about how to tell his parents he must go to the City that he had no heart for eating. At last, when the others had scraped their plates clean and his mother got up to make the tea, Robert said:

"I'm going to the City tomorrow."

There was complete silence. Then Robert's father began to laugh.

"That's a good one."

"I mean it," said Robert.

His father's sea-burnished face turned crimson. His brothers looked at each other. His mother put down the kettle with a thump.

"You've been talking to that old woman again, haven't you?" she demanded. "You always come back from her with your head stuffed with nonsense."

"It isn't nonsense," said Robert. "She told me the City is seeking me. I have to go."

His father pushed back his chair and stood up.

"I've heard enough of this!" he shouted. "There isn't any City, Robert. You know it's only a story."

Robert stood up too. His heart was beating fast.

"You say it's only a story. But I know it isn't. Last night I saw a picture in a dream. Granny Fishbone said it was a mosaic in the king's palace. She knows all about the City, Dad. She's a Witch Woman."

His father gripped the back of the chair.

"Witch Women don't exist," he said. "And if Granny Fishbone is your idea of one, Robert, then you're as mad as she is."

"All right," said Robert. "All right! If we're mad, where did this come from?" He reached inside his shirt and pulled out the silver fish. "No one here could make such a thing. It came from the City and I'm going to take it back."

For once his father had nothing to say. His brothers could not take their eyes off the little fish, while his mother stared at Robert with a troubled face.

"Maybe it did come from the City," she said at last. "Maybe there was a City once. My grandmother always told me so, and I loved her stories when I was a girl. But that doesn't mean there's anything to find now, Robert."

"What does it matter where it comes from?" his brother John demanded. "You'll be leaving school soon, Robert, and helping us with the boat. You won't fish any better for knowing about the City."

"Maybe I won't," said Robert. "But I still have to find it." His face began to burn as he tried to explain. "You're happy, aren't you, John, fishing with Dad and Luke, and going to market once a week? You've never thought of doing any-thing else. But the stories are what I was born for! I can't shake them out of my head. I feel as if I'm part of them. Granny Fishbone says I'll see the story of the Witch King come true. If I get to the City, if I see him, I'll come back and tell you all. Then when you hear the story you'll be able to say, 'This happened. Robert saw it.' "

Nobody spoke for a long time. Then Robert's mother said:

"John, go upstairs and bring down your old knapsack."

"Don't tell me you're going to let him go!" cried Robert's father.

"We'll get no peace otherwise," said his mother. "He'll come home soon enough when he gets hungry."

But secretly she had begun to wonder if Robert might be right. Robert crossed the room and hugged her grate-fully.

"I know what road to take, so please don't worry," he told her. "And once I reach the kingdom I'll be met."

"I suppose the worst that can happen is that he'll catch cold sleeping in a damp field," John said at the foot of the stairs.

"And what do we tell the neighbors?" demanded his father, still in a rage.

"Tell them Robert's gone completely crazy," said Luke sourly. "You won't even be lying."

The next morning Robert woke so early that not even his father or brothers were up. It was still dark outside and the first shrill notes of birdsong were just beginning as he got dressed. His knapsack was packed and lay on top of his chest of drawers. He was setting out after breakfast. All that was left was to say his good-byes. He slipped quietly out of the house and began to walk along the beach as the dawn wind rose.

"You're going then, are you?" bellowed a voice behind him. Robert turned. He could just see the outline of Granny Fishbone's hat.

"I was hoping I'd find you here," he said. "Granny Fishbone, I wish I didn't feel so scared. I wish I could be certain I'd be safe."

"Do you think it's any safer here?" Granny Fishbone gave a hoot of laughter. "And you the son of a fisherman! A wave might carry you off as you stand on the beach, and the sea could tip you out of a boat as easy as winking."

"It's very good of you to come and say good-bye," said Robert, slightly offended.

"Nonsense," Granny Fishbone retorted. "You'll see me again sooner than you think." Robert did not dare ask her what she meant. Her boots shuffled on the sand. "Be careful, Robert," she added gruffly. She pulled out a large dirty handkerchief and blew her nose.

Robert smiled. "I'll try." Then he turned from her with a quick wave, and began to run back across the sand. Light was streaming from the open door of the cottage; framed in the doorway stood his parents looking out for him.

After breakfast Robert and his father set off down the white road that led west out of the village. When they reached the footpath south over the steep fields, Robert's father swung the knapsack he had been carrying for his son off his back.

"Get over the stile and I'll hand it to you," he said. "This is where we part company."

Robert nodded, but did not move.

"It'll be the talk of the village, won't it?" he said. "Luke will hate that."

"Luke will live it down and so will I," his father said. "Your mother is right. You ought to go. Only don't be ashamed of coming home when you find the City doesn't exist. You'll be able to deal with the real world then."

Robert said nothing. He turned away and began to climb the stile.

"Here you are, then." His father handed him the knapsack. As Robert took it, his father's hand came down upon his shoulder and gripped it hard.

"Come back safe," he said.

Then he was gone, and Robert set off as fast as he could southward across the sheep pasture.

FOUR

Rain dripped down the back of Robert's neck as he lay
in a corner of a ruined stone house. At the door, at every
gaping hole in the walls, it fell like a curtain of water,
shooting through the broken roof in great sluicing loads
as the wind swept across it. Robert huddled his body together under his wet coat and hugged himself. Finally, he
slept.

After leaving the road he had walked southwest across
the hilly pastures that stretched inland from the coast as far
to the west and to the south as anyone from Robert's village
had ever been. It was lonely countryside, where sheep
cropped the thin grass, and big black crows perched on the
stone walls that separated one farm from another. Smoke
rose from the chimneys of the distant farmsteads, but
Robert encountered no one as he walked.

Late on the first day the ground began to climb steeply.
The grass grew sparser, and bracken and springy heather
began to replace it. Robert spent the first two nights out on
the open moor, waking so often at the cries and movements
of nocturnal birds and small animals that it seemed as

though sleeping and waking had fused into a third state, where he saw and heard the world through a film of dreams. He had woken stiff and light-headed, and deeply puzzled. Something was missing. It took him until drizzling noon on the third day to realize what it was. He could no longer hear the sea.

That discovery was soon followed by another. Across the moor at regular intervals Robert kept coming upon gray stones, shaped like tombstones only smaller, half hidden by the heather. When he bent down to examine one, his fingers could tell that it was a milestone. Where he was walking had once been a road. The bracken was less thick here, and sometimes he saw broken remains of stone paving. And once he came across a piece of harness, almost rotted away, its buckle corroded by rust. Robert stood for a few minutes, touching the thing gently with his foot, wondering who had abandoned it there and how long ago.

He spent the third night in the ruined house and when he woke at dawn the rain had stopped. Stiff and cold, he stumbled out into the morning air, and saw a track stretching like a wet brown ribbon ahead of him out of the moor. He pulled some hard bread and his flask of water out of his knapsack, and began to walk toward the track as he ate and drank. The sun warmed his back and legs as he walked, and his stiffness gradually eased. The track descended gently at first, then more steeply. The heather gave way to stunted woodland, copses of hawthorn and rowan tangled with bracken and bramble. Robert walked steadily until evening when the track descended into a green valley.

It was beautiful. Robert walked between rolling fields of

a richer green than he had ever seen, shaded by large trees through whose branches sloped the rays of the setting sun. Cattle stood calmly at the edge of a brook that marked the far boundary of the field on Robert's right. He had never seen hedges before and did not know whether men had made them or not. As he reached the bottom of the valley there came a curious tingling sensation in his feet and a rush of excitement into his heart. Robert knew that he had crossed into the kingdom. He wanted to shout and sing. He touched the hedges and laughed. He had arrived! The hardship of the journey was forgotten.

Straight ahead, a mile or so further down the track he saw a double row of cottages built out of fine gray stone. There, surely, was the place he would find a welcome if, as Granny Fishbone said, the City was seeking him. Robert hitched his knapsack more securely onto his back and set off toward the village.

As he passed the first cottage half a dozen dogs yelped in warning. Dusk had crept up behind him; a lamp moved behind the first window and he was surprised to notice how yellow and bright it appeared. Then the doors began to open down the street. Robert stopped, then walked on. The figures in the doorways held up lamps to distinguish him from the growing dark, and in their light Robert saw hostile eyes staring out at him in silence.

He began to grow afraid. He caught glimpses of faces, men's and women's, narrow and dark or soft and pink and spreading, but all with the same hard expression. Dogs growled at him from the shadows around the doors; only the whispered rebukes of their masters restrained them, and their eyes continued to follow Robert until he had come to the end of the village.

Bewildered, he threw himself down in a dry ditch with the wind rattling the hedge beside him, and stared up at the moon and the remoter stars. He had never felt so lonely. Perhaps Granny Fishbone was wrong, and the City was not seeking him. Perhaps he was mistaken, and this was not the kingdom at all but some other place, or, worst of all, perhaps there was no kingdom, no City to find.

But as Robert turned on his side and watched the long grass at the ditch's edge quiver, he again felt that sensation of tingling. It was as though the soil were declaring its nature to him. This *was* the kingdom. It was also clear that something was badly wrong.

He drifted into a fitful sleep and when he awoke at first light, he got up and turned to look back at the village. The gray stone seemed beautiful in the silence and early light. Robert began to walk on his way. Then, from behind the hedge to his left, there came a voice. Deep, unmusical and very tense, it asked:

"Would you like some breakfast, Robert Harding?"

FIVE

The voice belonged to a man who now stuck his head above the hedge. He wore a round black cap over short dark hair. His face was long and pale and he had several days' growth of beard. His eyes were green like a cat's, almond shaped and alert. His mouth was thin, the lips rather too firmly set. Robert could not guess his age.

"How do you know my name?" he demanded, a little frightened. "I don't know you."

The man smiled. "No? But perhaps I know you a little. My name's Godfrey."

He began to push his way, with some effort, through a narrow gap in the hedge.

Robert saw that he was tall and thin, dressed in a rust colored robe reaching nearly to the ground. He carried a sack.

"Are you sure you wouldn't like some breakfast?" he persisted. "I'm going to have some."

It dawned on Robert that this Godfrey was a traveler like himself.

"I didn't see you on the road last night," he said with a trace of suspicion.

Godfrey, who had sat down on the grass by the side of the road, laughed. "That's because I was coming from the south," he said.

Robert nodded inattentively, watching Godfrey take a loaf of bread and a lump of cheese out of his sack. Then the words trickled slowly through his mind again. *Coming from the south* . . . Suddenly he burst out: "You're from the City, aren't you? And you've come to fetch me. Why didn't you say so?"

Godfrey smiled a slow, rather cunning smile. "I have come to fetch you," he agreed. "I am the king's wizard, Godfrey the wizard, at your service."

Robert frowned. "What does a wizard do?" he demanded.

Godfrey's eyes grew hard and sparkling. "Think," he said in a tight voice. "Who keeps the City safe? Who chants the Words of Entry and interprets the Spell of Binding?"

"I don't know what you're talking about," Robert said uneasily. "What Spell?"

Godfrey plunged his hands deep into the pockets of his robe and looked about him. He began to whistle an intricate, trilling melody very fast, and then broke off abruptly, glanced at Robert and said:

"That does surprise me. Outsiders are obviously cut off from the Spell, but I had thought you would at least have heard of it."

"Well, I haven't," Robert replied rather resentfully.

Godfrey glanced back at the village, and got swiftly to his feet.

"Let's talk as we walk and eat as we talk," he suggested.

"It's time the villagers were up and about. I don't suppose you want to encounter them again?"

They set off briskly and after a few minutes hard walking had put a good distance between themselves and the village. Then Godfrey reached into his sack, broke off a large fragrant chunk of crusty bread and handed it to Robert. Robert thought it was the most beautiful bread he had ever tasted. He felt his toes curling inside his boots with happiness at the relief of his sharp hunger. Then Godfrey gave him another chunk of bread and a piece of yellow, savory-smelling cheese. As Robert ate, Godfrey talked.

"The Spell of Binding is the life of the City and the kingdom," he began. "Everything that has ever happened or will ever happen in the kingdom is included in the Spell. That doesn't mean the Spell controls what happens. It simply includes all the possibilities, all that the City might ever have been or might some day become, as well as the City that actually is."

"I see," said Robert. "At least, I think I see."

"Good," said Godfrey. "Now, we don't see the whole of the Spell because we're in it, if you understand. But I can say something called the Word of Entry that allows us to tap into the Spell and see what is immediately ahead. It's like a magnifying glass moving over a map."

"Or like standing on a hill and seeing a road stretch ahead?" Robert suggested.

Godfrey nodded. "Only, if you imagine not one road but a thousand, all branching off into other roads and still other roads again, you've got a better picture of it. And if you remember that none of the roads ahead actually exists until a wizard chooses to send someone down them, you'll have a better idea still."

Robert was silent, considering this.

"So that is your job?" he asked at last. "You choose which road the City takes among all those thousands?"

"That is my job. Or it was until something strange happened."

"What was that?"

"The Spell appears to have broken down," said Godfrey. "When I speak the Word of Entry all that I see is a confusion of images that make no kind of sense. They are followed by sudden and total darkness. Among those images was a name and a face—yours, Robert. It took us some time to guess you were an outsider, but when we realized that, the king sent me to find you."

"Because you saw me in the Spell?"

Godfrey nodded. "It makes very good sense to bring you to the City," he said, almost as if he were arguing with himself. "You are an outsider. Perhaps you can see where we are blind. We are part of the Spell, Robert, so how are we to judge what is the matter? And the need is urgent. We know from many other signs that a time of crisis is coming. The Witch King is coming and we do not know what he will bring."

"Yes we do," Robert retorted. "He'll restore the kingdom. The prophesies—"

"Oh, you know about the prophesies, do you?" Godfrey interrupted. "Curious, that: the prophesies, but not the Spell. Well, if you know the prophesies, you'll know how

ambiguous they are. 'He shall save the City yet destroy it.'
It is a terrifying prospect, Robert, and we must prepare ourselves to meet it. If we could only right the Spell, I should
feel more confident."

He fell silent, and looked so somber that Robert scarcely
liked to interrupt his thoughts, though he was full of questions. He did not understand how the Spell related to the
stories he knew of the City. Why hadn't Granny Fishbone
told him about it? They walked on in silence, Robert watching the scarlet poppies sway among the unripe grain as the
pasture gave way to ploughed fields and the hedges grew
thinner. Away to his right was another gray stone village,
shaded by trees, close to the winding river.

"I don't understand why those villagers were so hostile to
me," Robert said eventually. "Is it anything to do with the
Spell?"

"It might be," said Godfrey. "For centuries now, kings
and wizards have neglected to look any further than the
City's gates. So long as the City's wants were supplied, they
were content. As a result, the name of the City and the
knowledge of the kingdom has almost been forgotten, not
only outside the kingdom but in its outlying regions.
Villages like Spitstone, where you had such an unpleasant
reception, have been virtually independent for generations."
He smiled rather ruefully. "They're none too friendly to
travelers coming from the south, as the teeth marks in my
left ankle testify. I was nursing my injured dignity in a cow
pasture when I saw you arrive."

"So you don't know why the kingdom has declined?"
Robert asked.

"The chronicles simply record the fact of it," replied Godfrey. "Some believe the laziness and complacency of our kings is entirely responsible. I think some greater force is at work. But what is certain is that now the very life of the City, the Spell itself, is under threat and I must fight to recover it with all my skill and power."

They continued in silence for some time. The sun climbed the sky and began to beat down on them from overhead. White dust rose up from the empty track as they walked, making Robert cough until his throat was dry and sore. The blackbirds in the hedgerow grew sleepy with the heat and some laborers on the far side of a cornfield lounged in the shade of a crooked oak, sharing a flask and eating bread and cheese.

"How far have we got to go before we reach the City?" Robert inquired.

"Several days' journey at the least," Godfrey replied. "We have some hard walking ahead of us. Now I've found you there's no time to be lost. I hope you have strong legs, Robert Harding!"

The afternoon wore on and Robert grew weary. The wizard walked at a much faster pace than the boy was used to, and he did not seem to need any rest. Cornfields alternated monotonously with barley fields, with the occasional bit of pasture for a tethered goat or a pair of horses.

They encountered surprisingly little traffic, only a couple of laborers walking home early, and a man with a small covered wagon, who seemed to be the local carrier. They stared at Godfrey and Godfrey stared back with catlike indifference, while Robert found himself blushing self-consciously. At last, when Robert could hardly walk another step, he turned to Godfrey and asked:

"Will we be stopping for the night soon?"

Godfrey stopped and stared at him with an air of surprise.

"We are in a hurry," he said. "I was expecting to reach the top of the chalk downs before it got too dark."

Robert stared at the road ahead and then back at the wizard.

"You're mad," he said. "That must be another ten miles, and most of it uphill. It will be dusk in an hour. How can we possibly do it?"

Godfrey shrugged. "I can't carry you. But I can make you forget the ache in your back and your legs. I can make you walk as I walk."

"All right," said Robert.

Godfrey began to tell a story. With the first word something strange happened inside Robert's head. He heard Godfrey's monotonous, slightly grating voice, but he also saw what was spoken of. It was stronger than a daydream, not quite like being asleep. Birds flew through the images, the sky began to darken behind them, and Robert still felt the ache of his body faintly. But he walked without noticing that he walked, absorbed in Godfrey's story.

He saw a king crossing the sea in a tall-masted ship, and landing on the western coast of the kingdom with his band of wizards. He saw his scarlet-cloaked soldiers fighting with the hordes of the robber baron who was ravaging all the land. He saw peace made, and the peace sealed by the marriage of the king to the robber baron's sister. Then he saw the kingdom founded and the City built, the wizards singing it into existence by the Spell of Binding. At that point Robert protested and began struggling to throw off the images.

"You've got the story wrong, Godfrey," he said. "The City was built from the tree, not through your Spell." His head ached horribly as the images left him staring into the empty dusk.

"Of course the City was built by the Spell," retorted Godfrey. "I thought I had made that clear. How else could everything that has ever happened in the City be included in it?"

"But—" Robert shook his head hopelessly. He felt too tired to argue. "They tell a different story in my village," was all he could say. "Yours makes my head hurt."

Godfrey fixed him with a green-eyed stare. Then he gave a short cold laugh. "I will tell you no more stories until we reach the City," he said.

They walked on in silence until they reached the brow of the rise. The moon shone strongly overhead as they lay down on the cropped slope beside the track, Robert rolled up in a blanket and Godfrey in his cloak. The next morning they continued their journey through the chalk hills. Robert toiled at the side of the silent wizard, seeing nothing for miles but sheep and grass and exposed, chalky soil. Godfrey made no reference to their dispute and Robert dared not mention it. He marched under the gray sky, with the wind whistling into his face, and wondered what he ought to do. A wizard of the City had not heard that the City had been built out of the tree. It made no sense at all.

They halted at dusk within sight of a lighted farmhouse,

ate and lay down to sleep. The quiet breathing of Godfrey beside him only increased Robert's loneliness, but in the morning the wizard turned to him with an eager smile, as though he had forgotten they had quarreled.

"We shall be down among the wheat fields in a few hours," he said. "It shouldn't take us more than a couple of days to reach the City from there. The road is busy, and we should be able to beg a lift."

Robert responded with a rather watery grin, but as they came down out of the hills he began to grow more cheerful. The country spread out below was beautiful. From the height of the last hill it looked like a giant patchwork quilt thrown down over a rippling mattress. Pale wheat fields and dark green pastures, woodland and water meadows formed broad irregular patches bordered by hedges. Through it wound a slow shining river from northwest to southeast. There were many villages, built out of pale golden stone, and where the road crossed the river there was a larger settlement. Robert peered into the distance, hoping for a glimpse of the City, but the ground rose a little and the view ended in woodland.

Once they had entered the valley it struck Robert forcibly that there were many more people about than he was used to seeing, even at home. They passed men mending hedges, driving cattle, and working in large numbers in the well-tended fields. In one village a whole crowd of children and other idlers were standing outside a blacksmith's shop, watching a reddish horse being fitted with new shoes.

No one paid Robert or Godfrey much attention, largely because they were now sharing the road with many other travelers, from farm boys whistling at the seats of carts full of cabbages and leeks for the local market, to drivers with strings of packhorses carrying cloth to the City's tailors. It was easy enough to get lifts from the lumbering farm wagons. They traveled from village to village in this fashion, until on the tenth morning of Robert's journey, an hour before dawn, he and Godfrey climbed into a cart that was taking vegetables to a City market.

Robert was too exhausted for excitement. He had spent the short night wrapped up in his blanket in a cow field, and he was certain he had not even dozed. He now crouched uncomfortably between cabbage-smelling sacks, jolted by the cart's iron-bound wheels as they ground over loose stones. The first faint signs of dawn lighted the blue-black sky and the birds began to sing. Robert heard the driver murmur to his horse, and remembered the man's clumsy bows to Godfrey and his attempts to make him sit in front beside him. The closer they had got to the City, the more people had recognized the wizard. Godfrey had avoided village hospitality for the last two nights simply to keep his business to himself.

Robert must have dozed, for when his eyes opened again the sky was gray and he could see Godfrey's face half hidden in the folds of a blanket. The wizard's eyes were fixed on the road ahead. Suddenly he stood, allowing the blanket to fall from him, and he cried out softly. There was triumph and longing and a little fear in that cry. Robert, straining his eyes, saw far ahead the gate towers of the City.

SIX

Standing beside Godfrey in the cart Robert gazed at the City wall which stretched from east to west as far as his eyes could see. It was three times the height of a man, built of a close-grained sandstone that shone like gold as the sun rose over the open fields to the east. The gate was not yet open as they approached, but up on one of the gate towers Robert saw two watchmen silhouetted against the pale blue sky and he knew they must give the signal soon.

Immediately below them was a large crowd of foot travelers; apple-faced countrywomen in red shawls with baskets of eggs and flocks of geese; sleepy day-laborers with their trowels and shovels; peddlers with huge packs and vagabonds with none. Behind them waited a long line of wagons loaded with milk churns and cheeses, sacks of flour and tethered calves. As the cart beneath Robert reached the end of this line one of the watchmen raised a horn to his lips; the note rose thrillingly into the air and at once there was a groaning of bolts and the iron-studded gate swung open. Godfrey turned to Robert and clapped his hand down on the boy's shoulder. His green eyes shone with a fierce joy.

"Let's get down," he said. "We should enter the City on foot."

Robert almost fell as he climbed down from the cart. His legs were trembling as he walked past the slowly moving wagons and he felt sick with anticipation. When he reached the gate he stopped and stood quite motionless. The laden carts lurched dangerously near him and the peddlers thrust past him impatiently, but Robert paid no heed. Before him the City lay open and for the present he was content simply to gaze.

The gate opened onto a wide street that ran directly south until it was lost in the distance. Immediately on either side was a row of shops and small houses cleanly built out of the same golden sandstone as the City's walls and decorated with a running frieze of birds hiding in thornbushes so skillfully carved that Robert could not take his eyes off it. Some of the wagons had stopped in the street and were being unloaded while tradesmen in striped aprons and shirt-sleeves took down shutters and put up awnings in preparation for the day's trade. Smoke was rising from chimneys all down the street and as the egg-wives and peddlers began to cry their wares they were joined by a dozen or more youths dressed in scarlet and blue who suddenly jumped down the front steps of different houses and set off at a run down the side-streets to the west.

"Apprentices," said Godfrey from behind Robert. "The stonemasons and the coppersmiths have their workshops in the northwest quarter."

Robert nodded, and turned his head to look over the

housetops to the east. Soaring into the sky above a mass of
tall green trees were towers and pinnacles of dark red stone.

"Is that the king's palace?" he demanded breathlessly.

"The king's palace is a good hour's walk south across the
river as you will find out when we set off for it," Godfrey
replied in amusement. "Those are merely the towers of the
astronomers and the spires of the Great Library."

Robert stared at them in awed silence for a minute and
then turned his attention back to the street. Close at hand a
bedroom window had been thrown up and a girl leaned out
to watch the wagons pass. She began to sing in a high clear
voice that caused a shiver of delight to pass through Robert.
Gazing at the fine stonework bathed in early light, his ears
filled with singing and his lungs with the fresh green smell
of leaves, he thought the City could hardly have changed
since the young man built it so many centuries ago. He took
a deep breath and stepped proudly across the threshold.

Immediately he knew something was wrong. He felt
dizzy and distressed; he could not get his breath, for the air
was thick with something evil. He clutched Godfrey, who
bent over him in concern. After a minute or two the intensity of the spasm faded and Robert was well enough to stand
alone.

"Too much excitement and not enough breakfast," Godfrey suggested lightly, but his eyes searched Robert's face in
puzzled anxiety. After a moment's hesitation he added, "I
think you are sensitive to the presence of the Spell, Robert.
If so, I had better warn you not to be distressed if you see a
change in me. It's only that I am not so free here as I am

outside. Remember I am only the servant of the Spell, and its power is strongest here at the center." He grimaced wryly. "If you value the Spell you won't mind the loss."

Then he picked up his sack and began to stride purposefully down the street. Robert stared after him, bewildered and distressed. What change, what loss did he mean? If it was caused by the Spell Robert was certain it could be nothing good.

Deep in thought, Robert scarcely heeded the sights and sounds around him as he crossed the City at Godfrey's heels. The first street led into a wider and busier thoroughfare, lined with trees and leading down to the river that crossed the City in a broad and glittering curve from southeast to northwest. The quays and docks were of clean gray stone, well kept but almost deserted. Only one ship was moored within sight of the three-arched bridge by which they crossed.

Just south of the river another great thoroughfare crossed the streets, forming an open-sided square. Crowded around the fountain in the center was a rabble of hawkers and piemen, costermongers and fishwives, all bawling their wares in a hundred distinctive cries.

The morning was older now and the square was full of people in their strangely cut and brightly colored clothes, moving toward their work or from shop to stall, or simply idling in the sun. The noise and the bustle and the clash of smells rather overwhelmed Robert who drew nearer to Godfrey. As they moved together through the crowd many of those nearest to them abandoned their occupations when they saw Godfrey and bowed deeply. It troubled Robert that their faces showed no pleasure, scarcely even respect, but something much closer to fear. He turned to Godfrey to see his response and got a shock. There was indeed something to inspire terror there.

Since Robert had last looked at him, the wizard's face had grown older and sterner. The lines of sardonic humor had been wiped clean, leaving it white and set like a mask. Godfrey's green eyes, meeting Robert's appalled gaze with a look of faint inquiry, were remote and cold. This, then, was the change Godfrey had meant. Robert looked away again without speaking, heartsick.

After crossing a number of busy streets they left the crowd behind them at last and entered a long and pleasant avenue adorned with statues of the City's kings. At any other time they would have captured Robert's delighted attention, but now he scarcely troubled to look at them. The avenue ended in a stone arch furnished with a gate of twisted iron-work; beyond it Robert saw a broad drive sweeping through parkland, and beyond the trees, glimpses of high white towers shining in the sun.

As they approached the gate two burly men dressed in green and gold stepped forward and bowed very low. "Welcome back, my lord wizard," said the taller in a deep and pleasant voice.

He swung open the gate and walked with them through the park. Then Robert saw the palace in its full splendor. Its towers and pinnacles rose up, so white and fragile they looked as though they had been cut out of paper.

When they entered the palace another servant met them.

"I want to see the king at once," said Godfrey. "Is he in his chamber?"

The man nodded, and Godfrey walked so swiftly to the stairs that Robert had to run to keep up.

As the door of the king's chamber swung shut behind Godfrey's back, Robert felt grateful to be, at last, alone. He wondered whether Godfrey expected him to wait outside the door until he re-emerged. The wizard himself had given no hint; yet another sign of the change in him.

"Left you dangling, has he?" a voice behind inquired.

Robert whirled around. A large liveried fellow was resting his back against the opposite wall. It was the servant who had been standing outside the king's chamber when they arrived. The voice was warm and sympathetic, but Robert felt a little afraid of this man. As he swung away from the wall and came toward Robert he gave off a faintly animal smell. But the hint of brutishness was no more than a hint. The man was a pacified wolf. His thick hair was shiny and smooth, his jaws were clean shaven and his eyes sparkled with good humor. But when he got close to Robert he stopped and stared.

"You're the stranger we've been seeing in the Spell, aren't you?"

Robert remembered what Godfrey had told him on the journey.

"I suppose I am."

The man grinned. "Then they'll be hours yet. Didn't your new master tell you to get something to eat?"

Robert shook his head, wishing Godfrey had. The man jabbed toward the door with a thick forefinger.

"My name's Wolf," he said, "and I'm supposed to guard

that. I can send for you when the wizard comes out. These great lords don't care what any of us do as long as we are at their sides when they want us. Go on—explore a little."

He gave Robert directions on how to get to the kitchen and whom to ask for something to eat. Robert thanked him. Really he thought he ought to stay by the door, but he had eaten nothing all morning and still felt quite faint and ill. Perhaps Godfrey was right and food would help. Under the friendly gaze of the serving man he walked slowly around the corner in the direction of the stairs. He wandered along, hearing the polished wooden boards echo to his footsteps. On his left the gray stone wall was hung with brightly woven tapestries, and on his right a series of large square windows overlooked a garden that opened on to the park.

He descended the stairs into a large white-paneled hall and, following Wolf's instructions, found a door in the extreme right-hand corner and walked through it into a cool dark passage. Ahead he saw a large brick archway glowing with firelight and heard a clamor of voices and a rattling of pans. He quickened his pace, then there came a scream and a crash; a skinny girl in a flapping brown apron ran out of the archway toward him, pursued by an immensely fat woman clutching a ladle. Seeing Robert, the fat woman puffed to a halt and looked at him, wiping her hot red face.

"I've come to get something to eat," said Robert. "Wolf told me to ask Molly to see to it."

The cook broke into a smile so broad that Robert found himself smiling back happily.

"Wolf sent you to the right place," she said. "He knows I

keep a corner of my larder for them that can't wait till the next meal. Come along, my lad. Only you mustn't expect me to stop and talk. I've a dinner to get."

In less than no time Robert found himself sitting at the big scrubbed table in the middle of the kitchen with a jug of milk, a crusty loaf and a plate of cold roast beef large enough to feed a family of fishermen. As soon as she served him Molly rushed away to scold a servant boy and Robert was left to eat and drink and to look around. The kitchen was huge and hot and dark, lit by an immense fire in a fireplace that took up almost a whole wall.

In every corner kitchen maids and scullions chopped and stirred and pounded; as Molly rushed from one group to another the knives flew more frantically through the air, spoons whirled in a frenzy and pestle nearly broke mortar with enthusiastic grinding. Robert had just finished eating when Wolf came striding into the kitchen.

"There you are!" he said crossly. "Why didn't you tell me the king wanted to see you too? You'd better get upstairs double quick."

Robert did not stop to argue. He just ran.

SEVEN

"You are most welcome to the City, Robert."

Robert straightened up from his deep bow and blushed. When he had opened the door, breathless from running up the stairs, he had almost apologized and walked out again, convinced he had mistaken the room in his hurry. That little wrinkled man in a felt cap and slippers could not be the king! For half a minute Robert had stared at the child-sized figure huddled in the high-winged chair. His hair and beard were white and sparse, and the heavy sea-green robe he wore seemed to tire his thin arms, so transparently frail were they. The old man had turned toward the door, smiling inquiringly, and then Robert had noticed Godfrey in the shadows (for the room was very dark) and stumbled forward to make his bow.

There was a fire in the grate between the wizard and the king, making the room almost hotter than the kitchen. Despite the sunshine outside, the blinds were drawn, so that the room resembled Granny Fishbone's hut on a chilly night.

"Won't you sit down, Robert?" the sweet old voice continued.

Robert did not obey at once but glanced across at God-frey. He was standing in the dim alcove beyond the fireplace with his back to the lowered blinds. There was something terrible in his stillness and silence as he stood among the shadows. Robert shivered as he remembered how he had eaten bread and cheese out of a bag with Godfrey on the journey. Looking at him now, his face rigid and his eyes completely empty of expression, Robert felt like crying.

"Forgive me if this room is uncomfortable for you," the king said, misinterpreting Robert's unease. "I am unwell and this is the climate my physicians recommend. It makes me feel like a boiled egg," he added with a smile to Godfrey.

The wizard's thin grin, acknowledging the joke, seemed to come from a distance of years.

Robert turned his eyes hastily toward the king.

"I'm sorry you had to send after me," he said, backing nervously toward a chair. "I didn't know you wanted to see me, or I would have stayed."

The king shook his head. "I'm glad you had the good sense to forage for yourself." He glanced across at Godfrey a little wryly. "Guests should not be left to dance attendance at a closed door."

"Oh, I didn't mind," Robert said. "I was happy to have the chance to explore." He began to stroke the thick velvet pile of the chair arm with his fingers, then stopped guiltily when he remembered how dirty his hands were. The king fixed him with a pleasant but penetrating stare.

"The City must feel very strange to you, coming from outside."

"It's very beautiful," Robert replied shyly.

The king nodded kindly.

"I believe Godfrey has told you about the Spell and that we want your help as an outsider."

"Yes," said Robert. "But I don't really understand. How can I tell you what the matter is? I don't even see why you have a Spell at all." He saw the king and wizard exchange glances. He blushed and continued hastily:

"I just mean I don't see why the Spell is such a good thing. When we came into the City, the air nearly choked me. I'm sure it's the Spell. It's as though it's a sort of poison, and not just to me." His eyes slid involuntarily to Godfrey.

"Wizards pay a heavy price for their power," the king replied with a sad sternness. "Robert, I do not wish to dismiss your words lightly, but it is clear you have not yet realized how important the Spell is to us. It is not just our future but our past. We cannot look beyond it. When the first wizards sang, they formed the City in all its possible forms. Can you really expect me to set against the Spell one outsider's anxiety and discomfort, and conclude that the Spell is rotten? Surely all you are feeling is the flaw in the Spell which we are seeking to mend?"

Robert lowered his head. "The Spell doesn't fit in with the stories," he said in a low stubborn voice. "It isn't the Spell that made the City. It isn't the Spell that needs renewing. It's the song the young man sang as he cut down the tree, and the scent of the tree's leaves."

The king could not help smiling a little at Robert's hot and angry face.

"What is this about a tree?" he asked. "What young man?"

"You must know the story of the tree," Robert said with mounting panic. "Everyone knows it."

"Everyone outside, perhaps," the king reminded him gently. "It seems your people have stories about the City that the City itself has never heard of. And yet they have forgotten the most important story of all, how King Leo and his wizards founded the City by the Spell."

Robert jumped to his feet. He could hardly believe what he had just heard. White and trembling he turned to the wizard.

"That's the story you told me on the way here! But you didn't say King *Leo* was supposed to have founded the City!"

"If I didn't I should have," Godfrey replied.

"But he was the wickedest king in the City's history!" Robert shouted. "Don't you know any of your own stories? King Leo was a traitor and murderer. You can't expect me to believe—"

"Robert, Robert!" The king held up a blue-veined hand. "Calm yourself. Sit down, please, and listen a moment." Reluctantly Robert obeyed, with a last furious look at Godfrey.

"King Leo was neither a traitor nor a murderer," the king said. "I am shocked you should have heard such a thing. Perhaps later I will ask you to tell me the tale, though I cannot believe it has any connection with the founder of the City. I am much more interested in your story about the tree. Will you tell it to me now?"

So Robert told him about the tree, and about the seed that had been kept to renew the City. When he had finished, the king said quietly:

"So you say the City was made by the young man from the tree, instead of by King Leo through the Spell. This is very strange! And where is the seed from which the new tree will grow?"

"The Witch King must have it," Robert said. "He is the one who will plant it."

"The prophesy cannot mean a real seed," Godfrey said at once. "This story of a tree isn't mentioned in any of the chronicles. No one here has ever heard of it. You had better put all that village nonsense out of your head."

"I think we are being a little hard on Robert," said the king. "We asked him to tell us what he knew, after all. We can hardly blame him if we do not like it! And his story of the tree attracts me, I do not know why."

He gazed hard at Robert, as if seeking the answer in his face.

"It does not attract me," Godfrey said. "Why not admit the truth? Robert is no use to us at all."

Robert stared at him in dismay. "But you brought me here! You wanted me to come!"

"He did, and he was right," the king said. "Robert, I do not understand what you have told us today. But if you learn more about the City and its ways, perhaps you will see how the Spell fits in with the stories from outside, and be able to help us. Altogether I think the best plan is that you, Godfrey, should take him as a pupil."

Godfrey bowed with thinly concealed discontent, and Robert's eyes sought the king's in mute appeal. Gently the king shook his head.

"You must learn about the Spell and the City," he said.

"What better way to do it? Godfrey, will you tell Robert his duties?"

"Very well," said Godfrey. "Robert, I expect you to come to my study every morning immediately after breakfast. You will sweep the floor and open the windows and see that everything is tidy. I don't allow servants in my study, and I always keep it locked. There are books and manuscripts which might be dangerous in the wrong hands. When you are there alone I expect you to lock yourself in and admit no one. Do you understand?"

Robert nodded.

"I will provide you with a key and with the clothes a wizard's pupil ought to wear," Godfrey continued. "And, since the king wishes it, I will teach you about the City and about the Spell."

The king now sat heavily back in his chair as though he was exhausted. Little beads of sweat had broken out on his forehead just below the rim of his embroidered cap. He drank a little water, and as Robert turned to him with a look of concern in his dark eyes, he smiled and exclaimed:

"Come now, Godfrey! At least admit you will be glad to have a pupil again!" Glancing at Robert, he explained, "The number of wizards has fallen greatly in our time. Godfrey is now the only one. My grandson, David, studied under him for a few years, but of course he could not become a wizard."

"Why not?" asked Robert.

"It is not permitted that a man should be both king and wizard. David has studied the Spell and wizardry only to learn as much as a future king must know." The king shut his eyes for a moment. "David's father, my only son, died in the great sickness that swept through the City ten years ago. David was not much older than you. He lost both parents, and for a long time we thought he would lose his young sister too. But Sophie recovered, and David has looked after her ever since. You could almost say he brought her up. He's a good ten years older then she is."

"He was an apt pupil," Godfrey said. "He would have made an excellent wizard."

The king smiled with great warmth. "Even Godfrey thinks that David is—special. Sometimes, Godfrey knows, I speculate about David and the prophesies."

"Perhaps it will be David," Godfrey said. "All we know is that it will be soon."

As the wizard spoke a long note began to boom through the corridors of the palace.

"We have talked away the whole afternoon," said the king. "You must come to me another day, Robert, and tell me this story of yours about King Leo." He got stiffly to his feet. "That sound is the signal to summon all my household. Every day at this time, if there is a wizard here to say it, the Word of Entry is spoken and the Spell is opened up for us to see." He took a step forward, and Godfrey moved swiftly to offer his arm as a crutch. As Robert followed them to the door, the king turned his head and smiled.

"You will see the puzzle for yourself," he said. "I wonder what you will make of it."

EIGHT

The white-paneled hall was full of people as the king descended the stairs, leaning heavily on Godfrey's arm. Robert, following behind, could pick out the serving men by their green and gold livery, but the rest formed an indistinguishable, brightly-colored mass. As the king began very slowly to cross the hall toward a pair of white and gold doors thrown open at the far end, the crowd first parted, and then began to follow after him in a cramped slow procession.

The sight of the packed hall rather unnerved Robert. As he hesitated on the last step of the stairs, a company of silk-clad courtiers stepped around him and came between him and the king. He experienced a moment of pure panic. Surrounded by strangers, with the Spell about to be invoked, his last shred of security had been snatched away. He clutched at the banister and peered desperately through the crowd, searching in vain for another glimpse of the king. A long fanfare of trumpets began in the hall beyond the open doors.

"Aren't you coming?" inquired a voice at his right. It

was Wolf the serving man, smiling in his slightly aggressive manner. Robert's fear collapsed at the sight of his familiar face. He turned to Wolf with a grateful smile and they passed through the white hall together into the room beyond.

There was a good deal more space there. While the nobles continued to move forward, Wolf took Robert's arm and steered him toward the back wall. As Robert lifted his gaze to look for the king again, he let out an abrupt gasp of astonishment. The far wall of the hall was completely covered in a pattern of stones, green and violet and black, mimicking the chaos of a stormy sea. It was the picture he had dreamed of in the village, the mosaic Granny Fishbone had told him had been made when the prophesies of the Witch King were written.

Wolf grinned and nudged Robert in the ribs.

"I can see you didn't expect that," he said. "They call this the Sea Chamber on account of it. I've never seen the sea myself, but if it's anything like that I don't think I want to."

Robert nodded distractedly, his eyes still on the mosaic. It was an awesome piece of work, but Robert was not frightened by it now. Granny Fishbone had said the mosaic had a special power that would come into its own when the Witch King had need of it.

The hall was now full and the crowd silently attentive. At the far end Robert saw Godfrey and a short red-haired young man dressed in black assist the king up some steps on to a dais. As soon as the king was seated on a large carved oak chair, the trumpeters behind him sounded a flourish and the king began a speech formally welcoming Godfrey back to the City. His voice was thin but very clear. While he was speaking, rather to Robert's annoyance, Wolf tugged his sleeve.

"Look behind us," he whispered.

Robert looked. A tall girl of about sixteen was standing in the open doorway, breathing hard as though she had been running. She had long honey-colored hair, tied back from an oval face, and she wore a green dress with a dull rich sheen. Her hazel eyes were fixed watchfully on the platform, and as the king's speech came to an end, she stepped forward, squaring her shoulders as if she found walking through the crowded hall an ordeal.

"Who is she?" Robert asked, gazing after her. He thought she was the most beautiful girl he had ever seen.

"That's Princess Sophie," replied Wolf in the same hoarse whisper. "She must have come back from the Great Library. She spends a lot of time there listening to the scholars or arguing with the astronomers. They say she's very clever. All this—" he swept an arm to indicate the crowded hall, "must've taken her by surprise. We didn't expect the wizard back so soon." He paused, watching Sophie taking her place on the platform beside the youth in black. "That's her brother, the one with red hair. Prince David. No one knows quite what to make of him. He's more than half a wizard. He'll be a powerful king."

Robert peered forward at the red-haired prince with considerable excitement. Perhaps David's grandfather was right to think he might be the Witch King. But how could David have the blood of the Witch Women in his veins? Then he saw Godfrey step forward to the edge of the dais and his heart began to thump violently. This was the moment he had been dreading. Godfrey was about to say the Word of Entry to the Spell.

The wizard raised his arms and began to chant in a voice that filled every part of the hall. The words were unknown to Robert yet he felt something quicken inside him. It was alien, it was forcing itself upon him, it made him feel sick; but the wizard's chant battered against his resistance, wearing him down, until at last he yielded and the words rushed through him and Robert was engulfed. He did not hear any more. He saw. Where Godfrey had been standing a moment before there was a boy dressed in black with a white unhappy face. Robert gazed at him for some moments before he realized with a sickening jolt that the boy was himself. There was something peculiarly horrible about watching himself speaking and gesturing with a desperate urgency, and not understanding the emergency. Suddenly the picture expanded to include Prince David and Wolf; some sort of struggle was taking place. He caught his own name being called out, then abruptly he was gone and Prince David was alone, raising his hands in a gesture disturbingly like Godfrey's when he began to chant. Almost at once a wild series of images imposed themselves in quick succession over the prince's, stabbing at Robert's eyes. They filled him with a horror that made his stomach churn though he could make no sense of them. A crowned and bearded stranger with cold eyes stared directly (it seemed) into Robert's face. Princess Sophie lay in an uneasy sleep on a stretcher while beside her a tall woman, restrained by guards, shook her head wildly and struggled to be free. More images followed, so swift and confusing Robert could not retain them in his mind; then came a roaring followed by darkness. To Robert's profound relief the Spell had come to an end. When next he could see it was Wolf's face peering anxiously into his own that he saw.

"Are you all right?" Wolf demanded.

Robert nodded, swallowing hard.

"You look a bit white." Wolf gave a short laugh. "Gave you a shock, seeing yourself like that, didn't it?"

Robert said nothing. He thought Wolf looked a little pale himself.

The king, leaning on his grandson's arm, and the wizard were now descending from the dais and making their way to the doors. They passed quite close to Robert, though neither looked in his direction. He caught the wizard's low murmur:

"Again the same. What can it mean?" and he saw the king shake his head in reply, his face white and drawn. It was only after they had passed out of the doors and the crowd began to disperse that it occurred to Robert to wonder what he was supposed to do now. His head ached violently and he could feel the horror of the Spell persisting like an unpleasant taste on the tongue. He took a tentative step toward the doors, but a large hand came down on his shoulder and gripped it hard.

"Don't fret," said Wolf. "I have orders to look after you."

"Funny," said Wolf, pausing in the act of chewing at a chicken leg. "Funny we should see you in the images when you're an outsider and all."

Robert merely grunted. He was still feeling strange inside. He and Wolf should have been eating supper in the servants' hall, but Wolf had decided it would be too noisy and boisterous for Robert in his present rather fragile condition and had brought him to the kitchen instead. The place was very dark and quiet now, lit only by the smallest of fires in the great fireplace, in front of which Molly rocked herself drowsily while the kitchen cat crouched, purring, on her lap. Two kitchen maids yawned as they brought the dirty dishes back from the servants' hall. As Robert watched, one of them glanced swiftly at Molly's back, then began bundling some things off the dresser into a bag. He was just about to ask Wolf about it when the serving man began to speak.

"I just wish I knew what it all meant," Wolf muttered. "Things just get worse and worse."

Robert pushed away his unfinished pie and leaned back in his chair.

"How do you mean, worse and worse?" he asked.

"I'll tell you a story that might show you what the City's like," said Wolf. "I was sent with a message a couple of weeks ago to one of those big merchants' houses along Kings' March—you know, where the statues are?"

Robert nodded, remembering the statues and the high walls beyond.

"They let me through the outer gate into a courtyard. There were lime trees growing in the middle, and their blossoms had fallen over the paving stones, which were all blackened and scummy. As I was waiting for the answer to my message, I had a good look around. It all looked fine enough—until you got close up. Then you could see how the pillars were almost bitten through and how the stone facings were just crumbling away. One day soon there'll be a crash and a roar and the whole place will fall down into dust and rubble. Yet from inside the house I could hear music and voices and laughter." There was a pause and then Wolf laughed. "The master of that house has a pretty penny, too, you may be sure. Perhaps it's just that all of us have got crooked and lazy. Take this place," he gestured behind him at the kitchen. "The king's steward buys his flour from a miller who adds chalk to it, and they both profit. The king's baker knows, of course, but doesn't complain. And the other servants steal whatever they can lay their hands on." Robert remembered what he had just seen.

"Not Molly," he said.

"Of course not Molly," Wolf replied. "I didn't say things were hopeless, did I? But when the Witch King comes he'll have a lot to put straight." He laughed again, and the sound came out unpleasantly like a snarl. "Maybe Prince David is the Witch King, as some people say. It would serve us right if he was. He'd enjoy fulfilling that second prophesy, all right. He'd destroy the City to save it."

Robert shivered. "Whatever do you mean?"

"I know he's the apple of the king's eye," said Wolf, "and he's even warmed himself a corner of Godfrey's chilly heart, but there's something not quite straight about him." He met Robert's wide stare with an irritable frown. "I can't put it any stronger than that. It's not as if he's *done* anything."

He snapped shut his pocketknife and stood up to go. Robert followed in a daze. Wolf took a candle from the box

by the door, lit it, and then led Robert through corridors
and upstairs to the room which was to be his own.

Wolf grinned and opened the door of the room. "I cannot
see much of you tomorrow. No candle left, that's typical.
You'd better have this one—I can find my way in the dark."

Robert thanked him faintly. Wolf's teeth gleamed in the
candlelight, and he was gone.

NINE

When Robert opened his eyes in the morning, the first thing he saw was a suit of black robes laid out on a chair beside his bed, with a key on top of them. He leaped out of bed and struggled into his new clothes. They added so much to his shyness that he got through breakfast in the servants' hall without saying a word to anyone. He found his way to Godfrey's room and let himself in, after knocking twice to be quite sure the wizard was out.

The study was a cold room, high up above the king's apartment. The walls were of unplastered gray stone, their sole ornament an illuminated text in a strange alphabet with an initial letter that writhed like a serpent in red and gold. Robert found a broom in one of the cupboards and swept the floor as he had been told. The early light was streaming in through the pointed window he had opened, and fell across the dusty cases of books and manuscripts. Robert was filled with a queasy delight as he thought of the power and knowledge concentrated in them. He found himself drawn to a particular book on one of the highest shelves, a large volume in a faded black and red binding. His fingers had hardly curled around the spine when a voice from behind him made his heart leap and the blood rush to his face.

"A dangerous choice of book, Robert Harding."

Godfrey had entered the room on soundless feet and stood by the door, his face guarded and his eyes watchful. Robert was too abashed to ask him what he meant. He moved away from the bookcase as though he had been stung.

The wizard seated himself behind a large black desk, and summoned Robert to his side with a curt gesture.

"Since I must take you as a pupil, I shall treat you like any other," he said. "The king wants you to learn about the City; very well. We shall begin with the City's history from the earliest times."

He began to speak about the reign of King Leo, during which trade expanded with regions outside the kingdom, great tracts were written by wizards and scholars and nobles performed many feats of splendid heroism. After about a quarter of an hour he broke off and stared coldly at Robert's dismayed and baffled face.

"You'd better write down the titles of a few books. I can see you're not taking this in. I shall expect you to know something about King Leo by tomorrow."

"I already know plenty," Robert muttered to himself, but out loud he said merely, "I thought you were going to teach me what wizards know."

Godfrey smiled thinly. "Wizards know rather a lot. I am going to teach you only the beginnings of their knowledge."

He continued to talk about King Leo for over an hour, making reference to several chronicles and a number of scholarly accounts. Eventually Robert conceded defeat and

took up a pencil and a bit of paper from the desk and began
to jot things down as best he might. Daydreaming his way
through school had hardly prepared him for this onslaught
and by the end of it he was hot and tired and desperate to
escape.

"You can find most of the accounts I mentioned in the
Great Library," Godfrey concluded, leaning back in his
chair. "That will give you a marvelous excuse to wander
through the City and waste time."

Robert left him, determined to go straight to the Great
Library and look at the chronicles Godfrey had mentioned.
But once he got out into the open air, crossing the park into
Kings' March, he inevitably slowed down. Passing the high
walls of the merchants' houses he remembered what Wolf
had said about the decaying buildings. He stared up at a
fresco eroded by time and neglect into faint unmeaning
shapes, and thought of Godfrey's life, walled up behind the
Spell. His anger left him, and he walked on in a somber
mood.

He began to cross the big square where the food stalls
clustered around the fountain and the smell of cooking rose
deliciously from the shops on all four sides. He made his
way with considerable difficulty, for the crowd was very
thick. He began to feel strangely oppressed, as though the
crowd pressing around him was squeezing the life out of
him.

Staring about him, Robert noticed what had escaped him
yesterday, that for all the noise and bustle in the square
remarkably little trading was being done. People scurried
about in their brightly colored clothes, tradesmen bawled

and the bakery chimneys smoked, but beneath the appearance of exuberant activity Robert suddenly saw there was a vacuum. For a moment it seemed as though he was standing among puppets, brightly dressed and animated figures jerked into action by an external force, without any thought or feeling of their own. Then the moment passed and the oppression lifted. Vitality returned to the faces of those around, warmth flooded the hawkers' cries, and Robert's panic left him. All the same he shivered. He was certain that what he had felt around him was the Spell, squeezing the life of the City as well as his own.

He reached the Great Library with such a feeling of relief that he was scarcely overawed by the magnificence of the long gallery in which he found himself. Frescoes of ancient poets and philosophers decorated the walls above rows of many thousands of books, which breathed a musty silence disturbed only by the pen scratchings of the scholars. Robert began to walk along the shelves, looking for the books he wanted, for he was much too shy to ask the grave old men bent over manuscripts at their desks, coughing hollowly in the dusty air. He walked the length of the gallery, turned a corner at the end, and found to his surprise Princess Sophie standing under a window with a heavy volume open in her hands, frowning down as she rapidly turned a page.

Robert turned red. He wanted very much to speak to her, but he did not know how to begin. Then he saw the title on the spine of her book.

"That's one of the books I wanted!" he exclaimed.

The princess glanced up at him briefly, and down at the

book again. Still half absorbed, she murmured reluctantly: "Then you'd better have it." But it was another minute before she shut the peeling brown covers and thrust the book into Robert's hands.

"Here you are." She looked at him properly this time. "Aren't you Godfrey's new pupil? The one from outside?"

Robert nodded, rather abashed.

The princess smiled, and her pale solemn oval of a face was transformed.

"I've always wanted to know what it was like outside." Her hazel eyes met his and held them. "When I was a little girl I thought I had only to set out by myself and look, but now I realize that that was much too simple."

Robert found himself smiling back. "I suppose a royal princess needs an escort of three hundred horsemen," he suggested shyly.

"At the very least." She tugged at a stray lock of hair, and began to wind it unconsciously around her finger. "I would like to hear you talk about your country. It might answer a few questions I have."

"About the City?" Robert asked hesitantly.

"About the City," she agreed. "And about other things that in there—" she nodded with her chin toward the book Robert held, "don't quite make sense." Her frown returned and Robert could almost have sworn a trace of fear crossed her face.

"I'd love to talk to you," he said simply.

She nodded, and half turned away as if she was regretting already the impulse that had made her speak.

"That's if my brother's business doesn't make it impossible," she murmured, and walked past him toward the door.

Robert found an empty desk and sat down with the book and tried to read. But the chronicle only contained the things Godfrey believed and expected him to learn, how King Leo founded the City with the Spell and what a wise and benevolent ruler he was. After a few pages Robert could not force himself to read any more. It was too disturbing. It raised the possibility that Godfrey might be right.

Instead he let his mind return to the princess. He liked her very much. And she was the first person he had met here who really cared about the outside. He turned a few more pages, remembering what she had said about things in this chronicle not making sense. Did she have doubts about King Leo or the Spell? It would be marvelous if she did. He shut his eyes for a moment, trying to remember what part of the book she had been reading when he saw her. It was quite close to the end. Robert began turning the pages rapidly. He cast his eyes eagerly down the closely printed columns and found himself reading a discussion of the prophesies of the Witch King.

"The Witch King shall come from the sea and return to the sea. He shall save the City yet destroy it. He is the bearer of the seed, planting the Tree for the City." The words Granny Fishbone had spoken returned to Robert as he read, and for the first time he began seriously to consider what the first of the sentences might mean. No wonder Princess Sophie sought an answer outside the kingdom! If the Witch King was to come from the sea, how could he possibly be City-born?

A thought crept into Robert's mind that slowly turned his face scarlet to the roots of his hair. He got up and fled out of the Library into the open air. All the way back to the palace the thought pursued him. Granny Fishbone had called him a donkey. Now the thing seemed staggeringly obvious to him, yet he continued to resist it. *He* had come from the sea, and hoped to return there. *He* had arrived at the expected hour. Most striking of all, only he in the whole of the City seemed to be aware of the necessity of getting rid of the Spell and planting the seed of the Tree for a new beginning.

"But it *can't* be me," he protested to himself, halting under one of the statues along Kings' March. "I'm not a king. And I'm not descended from a Witch Woman."

He ran through the gates into the park and slipped inside the palace by a side door close to the kitchen and the stable yard. As he climbed the stairs to his room a thought struck him.

"If I'm the Witch King, why haven't I got the seed of the Tree?" He flung open the door of his room, intending to throw himself down onto the bed in relief, when he realized that he had a visitor.

"Hello, Wolf," he said cheerfully. "What are you doing here?"

Wolf rose from the chair by the window.

"Prince David's page came looking for you. I said I'd pass this on." He held out a white paper, folded and sealed, and watched rather anxiously as Robert turned it over. "It's the prince's seal," he said. "And his handwriting."

Robert nodded, broke the seal, and began to read.

"He wants to see me in his rooms!" he exclaimed. "To-night." He looked up at Wolf in astonishment.

"Tell Godfrey," Wolf advised. "Ask him what you should do."

Robert blushed slightly. The memory of that morning's lesson still rankled.

"Why should I?" he demanded. "I'm not a child. If the prince wants to see me, that's my—"

"Don't be a fool!" Wolf snapped. "Prince David doesn't invite the likes of you or me around to his private apartment unless he *wants* something." Seeing Robert's jaw set stubbornly, he sighed and softened his tone, trying to smile. "He usually gets it, too. He's got a lot of charm. Maybe I'm being over hasty, Robert. All the same—if it was me, I'd tell the wizard."

Robert frowned and re-read the paper in his hand. "I don't think I can do that," he said.

Robert's thoughts were agitated as he made his way along the dim passage toward Prince David's apartment. He had to be cautious, he knew; Wolf's warning had not gone unheeded. But after that letter he could no more have kept away from the prince than he could have turned back from the City gates after a glimpse inside. For after warning him of the need for absolute secrecy, the prince had summoned him to a meeting with the Witch King.

TEN

As the guard who waited outside the prince's door went to announce him, Robert wondered whether the princess was also to be present at this meeting. She had said her brother's business might make it impossible for her to talk to him. Was this what she had meant?

The guard returned and swung open the heavy oak door. Robert stepped inside. All he registered for the first few seconds was a feeling of space and the sensation of cool and scented air upon his face, for the blaze of candlelight dazzled him after the dimness of the passage. When his eyes had adjusted he saw Princess Sophie seated on a heavily carved couch across the room. She was sitting tensely upright, her hands clasping a piece of embroidery. Skeins of the colored silk she was using for the work fanned out across the lap of her blue velvet dress. Robert was very glad to see her. She looked up as he approached and her face relaxed into a smile. Robert smiled back. Neither of them had managed to speak yet when a warm and delightful voice called across the room: "Robert! How very kind of you!"

It was the prince. He had been standing by the window

and now walked rapidly toward Robert. He was dressed in black and his hair shone red in the light. He was something under middle height and rather plump. There was a curious and very attractive contrast between the smooth confidence of his voice and the nervous excitement that blinked in his pale freckled face and his active hands. Robert attempted a clumsy bow, but the prince laughed pleasantly and waved it away.

"Please, no formalities. Come and sit down. My sister will pour us all something to drink."

It came out as a cross between a polite appeal and a command, just the tone Prince David might have used with a trusted servant. Flushing slightly, Princess Sophie rose to her feet and crossed to a table on which stood a jug of wine and some goblets. Robert did not like to protest, but the incident struck him unpleasantly. As if reading his thoughts, the prince smiled and met his eyes with a warm blue stare. It gave Robert quite a shock; nobody had ever looked at him so directly before. After a moment he found himself smiling back.

"I had to exclude servants from tonight's discussion," the prince said quietly, "so we must shift for ourselves, I'm afraid."

Robert nodded and sat down. When the princess brought him a goblet of wine he accepted it with no more than a friendly nod. The prince was absorbing all his attention.

"Shall we get to the point, then?" said David briskly, setting down his wine untouched. "Robert, who do you think is described by the prophesies of the Witch King?"

Robert was taken aback. He glanced from David to the

princess and around the room and realized, belatedly, the significance of the fact that only the three of them were present. It was David he had been summoned to meet. For the second time that day Robert blushed to the roots of his hair.

"The prophesies," reminded David gently.

Robert swallowed. He dared not admit he had applied them to himself. A deep shame began to spread through him that the thought had even entered his mind. Hadn't the king, hadn't even Godfrey suggested it might be David? Yet, running through the prophesies in his head, Robert found it hard to see how they might fit.

"I took the first prophesy quite literally," he said humbly. "The second, about destroying the City, I don't understand. The third, I thought referred to the village story that the first king built the City out of a tree and that a seed was kept to be planted by the Witch King when the City needed renewing."

Princess Sophie looked up, her hazel eyes appealing to Robert's with a curious expression mingling suspicion and hope.

"Why do we only have the prophesy and not that story?" she demanded. "You think that story's the true one, don't you?"

As Robert nodded, her face lit up. But Prince David began to laugh.

"A pretty fable!" he exclaimed in his pleasant voice. He came around the couch and sat down beside the princess. "My sister has a taste for tales like yours," he said. "However rigorous her intellectual training, her romantic imagination will break out." He sat forward. "Shall I interpret the prophesies for you, Robert?" David's smile was so gentle and his gaze so candid that Robert found himself staring.

"Let us consider the third prophesy first of all," Prince David was saying. "Isn't the Spell of Binding both the seed of the City and the tree, given to us by Leo the first king? It is the City in seed, the potential City, as well as the City as tree, the City in its full glory. But now, as we all know, something has gone wrong with the tree. It is blighted, possibly beyond recovery. We must recover the seed, Robert, the potential of the Spell, and grow a new City from it."

Rapt in the intensity of the prince's smile, Robert nevertheless stirred uneasily. "Leo wasn't the first king, and it's a real tree, not an image. It means the Tree in the story."

Prince David laughed delightedly. "Really, Robert! Next you'll be claiming that the Witch King will come to us from the seaside."

"He has to be a descendent of a Witch Woman," Robert said.

David smiled. "Where is that written? Show me."

Abashed, Robert hid his face behind his goblet, draining his wine to the dregs.

Prince David's voice recaptured him.

"The Witch King shall come from the sea and return to the sea. What can it mean? Surely not that a king shall come from outside the City, a stranger to the royal line!"

His stare had become a pale blue flame, compelling Robert's eyes. Hardly able to move his lips, the boy asked in a whisper, "Then what does it mean?"

"I was born in the Sea Chamber," David said. "My

mother had a fall and began her labor, and the doctors dared not have her moved. A rare accident, Robert; the only birth recorded there in the long history of my family. When the end comes, when I am dying, I will have my bed brought there, for the end should be in accordance with the beginning." He held his hand out to Robert. "I am he."

As Robert stared like a fool at the prince's hand, Sophie's voice cut urgently into his confusion.

"Do you believe it?" she demanded.

Robert looked up at her. Her expression was pleading and desperate; the color burned in her cheeks. She too was struggling for conviction. Was David the Witch King? Before Robert could answer her, David's voice cut in.

"Do you believe it?" the prince asked, as blithely as if only one answer were possible. And Robert gave it. He bent to kiss David's smooth white hand and the relief of surrender almost washed away the cold conviction of betrayal.

The next moment David was on his feet, refilling Robert's goblet.

"Now, to action," he said briskly. "The prophesy says I have to plant the seed. In other words I have to recover the beginning of the Spell and start again. That's where you can help me, Robert."

"I can?"

David nodded. "I need you to unlock Godfrey's study. When I was his pupil, he kept a particular book there, an old one with a black and red binding. It's that book I need. It explains how a man can say the Word of Entry in such a way as to get back to the beginning of the Spell. Think of it,

Robert! He'd be there with King Leo and the seven wizards, hearing the first words of the City's making!"

Robert wondered whether to object again. He looked up and saw that Sophie was staring at him, appealing to him to contradict her brother. Suddenly he felt very angry. His head was confused with wine and his will was exhausted. Why did she expect him to speak if she kept silent herself?

"Whoever went back would be in possession of the whole Spell before anything went wrong," David was saying. "Whoever heard it then and kept it would be able to plant it wherever he chose. He'd have complete power to right the City. It would be a new beginning. He would save the kingdom and restore the City to the height of its glory!"

Sophie was staring at her brother with a gaze of horror that seemed to Robert inexplicable. But when David smiled at her and stretched his hand to her she took it without protest. It was to Robert, however, that she spoke.

"Is that what the third prophesy means? Is it, Robert?"

Robert looked away and rubbed his forehead in confusion. He was out of his depth; more than anything in the world he wished this evening was over. He drank from his goblet and the wine warmed the cold place in his heart.

"David ought to know what the prophesy means," he said.

The prince gave a shout of delight and squeezed his sister's arm.

"What did I tell you, Sophie? The outsiders think the same as us!"

But Sophie bowed her head as if she had been condemned. Watching her, Robert suddenly felt deeply alarmed. It seemed as if in some way he could not understand he had decided her fate. It made part of him want to shout mad denials to David, seize her hand and escape with her out of the room. He didn't, of course.

"I need that book soon," David was saying. "Tomorrow night I know Godfrey will be with the king. He is attempting some spell to ease the king's sickness. Could you let me into his study then? It will be quite safe."

Robert nodded miserably. It was exactly what Godfrey had forbidden him to do. He found the prince was now helping him to his feet, and was surprised how unsteady his legs felt. The wine also seemed to have done something funny to his eyes. As he made his way uncertainly to the door, an objection to David's plan suddenly detached itself and floated to the surface of his mind.

"Godfrey said that book was dangerous. And you're not supposed to meddle with magic, are you? A king can't be a wizard."

David laughed. "But the Witch King can't be anything else," he said.

ELEVEN

Robert slept heavily that night and woke late. It was a chilly overcast day, and he hurried into his clothes. Breakfast would be long over, but Robert did not care much. Last night's strong wine had taken away his appetite. It was not only the wine, of course. He remembered the promise he had given to help David. A groan escaped him and he sat down abruptly on the bed.

What had he done? Robert felt horribly uncertain. In the gray morning light, without the prince's compelling presence to excuse them, Robert's words and actions returned to him like sorry ghosts. Last night he had been willing, for David, to abandon the stories Granny Fishbone had told him and to believe that the City began through the Spell. Last night he had promised to help David mend the Spell, when the one thing he had been sure of ever since he came to the City was that the Spell was evil. Robert rubbed his uncombed hair with a distracted hand. Which was the madness, what he had felt when he saw the prince, or what he believed once more in the prince's absence?

"If he isn't the Witch King, what *is* he?" Robert cried out. "Is it my fault if I wanted to believe him?"

Then he remembered Princess Sophie's look when he denied the village story of the seed, and the certainty of his guilt settled like lead around his heart.

"Why should *she* care so much?" he demanded in a hot rush of anger. "They're not her stories!"

But he knew, as he got to his feet, that the stories belonged to everyone in the City.

"All the same, a promise is a promise," he protested as he reached the door. "I'll have to help David. I can't get out of it." You could if you dared, a voice inside him replied. And instead of making his way to Godfrey's room for his lesson, Robert found himself crossing the palace to the king's apartment.

The king looked frailer than when Robert had seen him two days before, but his eyes, shining brightly in his wrinkled face, had lost none of their shrewdness.

"Something is troubling you, my young friend," he said as soon as Wolf had closed the door, leaving them alone together. "Come and sit down and tell me what it is."

He pointed to a low stool beside the fire. As Robert came forward and sat down, he noticed that the king was wearing an old pair of soft black slippers under his fine robe, slippers that any grandfather might wear. It comforted him and gave him courage.

"I don't know where to begin," he admitted.

The king looked at him and smiled. "Take any end and start to unravel it, and the whole tangle will begin to become plain."

Robert nodded. "Must I always keep a promise?" he asked hesitantly.

"There's a simple question!" exclaimed the king. "I suppose you want me to answer it with a plain yes or no?"

"Can't you?"

The king laughed. "If children had made the world, night would follow day in a wink and only good men would be happy. And there would be no long evenings for bad old men like me to enjoy." He laughed again, seeing the look of dismay on Robert's face. "Forgive me, Robert. I haven't gone quite mad. I will answer your question, but I cannot answer it simply. I can only say that it depends on the promise and the consequences of keeping it."

Robert nodded, swallowing his disappointment.

"Try to unravel another end, if that one didn't help," the king advised.

"All right," Robert said. "I'll try." He had to think carefully first. He could not risk breaking his promise to keep David's secret.

"Suppose," he began, "you read somewhere that it was possible to go back to the beginning of the Spell, and hear the whole thing as it was said for the first time. Suppose you read that it was possible to bring that knowledge back and use it to put the Spell right." He paused and then added, "Well, maybe you should help someone to do it. But if you're not sure the Spell is a good thing and if you're not sure what the person will find if they do go back, what should you do?"

"I understand the difficulty."

The king drew himself upright and stared at the fire for

some minutes without speaking. His veined and translucent hand beat softly upon the arm of his chair while he thought. As last he sighed and said abruptly:

"Robert, forgive me. I know you do not want to break a confidence, but you did not read about this idea in a book, did you?"

Robert blanched and sat very still.

"My grandson can be very persuasive," the king said. "And he has a specialized knowledge which I occasionally regret that he acquired. Why does he imagine that he knows better than Godfrey? If this scheme is written in one of Godfrey's books, it's a matter of purest speculation, the dangers unknown and the method untried." He clenched his hands upon the arms of his chair and as the knuckles whitened, Robert realized with a shock that he was extremely angry.

"If the method has not been tried it is because Godfrey has good reason not to try it," he continued. "I will speak to Prince David this afternoon. This business must go no further."

Then, to Robert's immense relief, he smiled. "Don't worry, I will see to it without eating David alive."

Robert laughed. Now that the king knew he felt as if a great burden had been lifted off his back. He felt a fleeting stab of guilt that he had not concealed David's plans better, but he could not pretend to be sorry. He had tried; his failure was due, he imagined, to the king's sharp insight. He was quite unaware of his tell-tale reference to "helping" someone.

"Was there anything else you wanted to tell me?" asked

the king. Robert shook his head. There seemed to be no need to tell the king that David might be the Witch King. At least he could keep one promise.

The king, meanwhile, was leaning back in his high-winged chair and gazing at Robert with great thoughtfulness.

"You haven't changed your mind about the Spell, have you?" he said. "David may have shaken you, but he hasn't convinced you. That impresses me very much. When you first arrived, Robert, I felt sure your dislike of the Spell was due to its strangeness. If your headaches and faintness had anything to do with the Spell at all, I thought they might be explained by its brokenness. But I am wondering now whether that explanation will do." He paused, then added, "There's too great a gap between your story of the beginning and ours to allow for both to be true. Either the Spell is the truth, or it is a lie. If it is a lie, no amount of mending will do. We must get rid of it."

"Get rid of it?" Robert echoed, startled.

"If need be," the king said grimly. "At our first meeting, Robert, you told me that King Leo was not the first king, but I gave you no chance to tell me the village story about him. I should like to hear that story now."

There was something so sad in the lines of the king's face that Robert reached out timidly and touched his hand. The king smiled.

"Don't worry, my young friend," he said. "All that matters in this is to find the truth, eh?"

Robert smiled back. Then he leaned forward on his stool, hugging his knees. His eyes focused on the memory of

Granny Fishbone's face. His ears listened to the rhythm of her words as she told the tale. He began the story. When he came to the murder of Leo's children, the king groaned aloud. Robert hurried on.

"When King Leo came to fetch his sons, he found Princess Judith in the nursery. She was dressing her dead children and singing to them. What had happened had sent her mad." Robert broke off and looked at the king. " 'The City's Shame,' they call that story at home. They say that Leo and Mark deserved one another but that the innocent deaths still cry out for vengeance."

"What happened to Leo?" demanded the king, grim-faced.

"Oh, he took another wife and had more sons. But because he was afraid that someone else could use the army just as he had, it's said he found a new way to guard himself and the City from its enemies, a secret way."

"A new and secret way to guard the City," murmured the king. His hands tightened suddenly on the arms of his chair and Robert saw from the set of his face that he was battling against pain. He jumped up, but the king shook his head.

"It always passes quickly. It's gone now." He smiled, but Robert saw that the spasm had left him shaken.

"A new and secret way to guard the City," he repeated, "long after the City had begun. Does that sound like the Spell? I wonder."

As Robert was gazing at him somberly the king gave a gentle laugh.

"You had better go and apologize to Godfrey for missing your lesson, my young friend. But first you had better find

a mirror. Your tunic buttons are fastened all wrong and
your hair makes you look like a hedgehog. I don't think
Godfrey will care much for that, do you?"

Robert squinted hastily down his front and began to
fumble with the buttons. When his tunic was buttoned right
he bowed to the king. Then he grinned.

"You're just like my mother," he said.

The king inclined his head.

"I am very glad to hear it," he replied. "Now, on your
way out, will you tell Wolf I have a message to send to the
prince? I think I had better see him without delay."

Robert left him then, very much happier than when he
had entered the room.

TWELVE

That evening after supper David's servant approached Robert as he was leaving the servants' hall.

"The prince will expect you in the place he mentioned last night," he said in a rapid undertone.

Though he did not understand the message he had brought, he enjoyed its effect on the wizard's boy. Robert turned white, as if he was about to be sick. The servant strolled away, and Robert stared after him in misery and dismay. Something had gone badly wrong. Not even the king had been able to stop David.

It did not occur to Robert to disobey the prince. He went straight to Godfrey's study and waited outside the door. As he stood in the candlelit passage he began to grow frightened. If the king had spoken to David, the prince must know that Robert had betrayed him. Robert dreaded what David might do. When he heard footsteps his heart began to pound, and he hardly dared turn around to face the prince.

But to his amazement David was smiling.

"Sorry I'm late," he said. "Are you ready to let me in?"

Thrown into confusion by his mild blue stare, Robert unlocked the door without a word.

The prince found the book he wanted and brought it to the lectern, where he began to turn the pages with maddening slowness.

"Please hurry, Prince David!" Robert cried, glancing at the open door in an agony of impatience.

"What's the excitement?" David murmured without looking up. "Godfrey isn't going to surprise us. He'll be with the king all evening. The old man wasn't even well enough to come to supper."

"I know, but . . ." Robert's voice trailed away. He was helpless.

"Here, Robert." The prince felt in his pocket and produced a note, waving it toward the boy without taking his eyes off the book. "I meant to send this to my sister earlier and forgot. Will you take it? And stay with her until I've finished, won't you? I really can't concentrate if you're going to sigh and fidget all the time."

Though it meant leaving the room unguarded, Robert took the note. He was eager to see Sophie again.

He left David standing among the shadows at the big lectern, with a candle held high over the red and black covered book, one finger running swiftly along the crooked script. Robert began to make his way across the palace toward the princess's apartment.

There was no guard at the princess's door and, at first, no answer to Robert's knock. When eventually the door opened it was Sophie herself who opened it. She was alone and she had evidently been crying. Her eyes were red and swollen and her oval face was blotchy. She blushed when she saw Robert in the doorway and her hand moved as if she wanted to shut the door again.

"I thought it was my brother," she said.

"Only his messenger," Robert replied. He hesitated, then added, "What's happened, princess? What's wrong?"

Sophie said nothing. She unfolded David's note, glanced at it, and crumpled it in her hand.

"Please, won't you come in?" she said. "I want to talk to you."

She turned and Robert followed her into the room. Tapestries of peacocks and firebirds glowed against the high white walls and, since the evening was cool, a fire burned pleasantly in the black grate. Two comfortable chairs stood on either side of it; the princess took one and, with a wave of her hand, invited Robert to take the other. For a long time neither spoke. The silence between them was tense and threatened to become unbreakable. The princess stared down at her clasped hands; she was frowning hard as if to prevent herself from crying again.

"What's the matter?" he asked. "Please tell me."

Her head shot up. "Why should you care?" she spat. Staring at her blazing eyes and the hard lines of her mouth, rigidly compressed to prevent it trembling, Robert realized with dismay that she was deadly angry. He didn't need to ask why. He knew. Suddenly he too lost his temper.

"He's your brother!" he shouted. "You can't stand up to him yourself!"

Sophie's face went dead. "I can't," she agreed in a flat voice. "But I thought—oh, Robert," she beat at the side of her chair with a despairing fist, "I thought for a moment there was some truth in those stories of yours."

Robert turned scarlet. In a very low voice he murmured: "There is. Of course there is, only—"

He raised his eyes and appealed to her.

"I know," she said. "I stop wanting to escape when I'm with him too."

For a minute they sat in silence again, each thinking of David. Then Sophie said:

"It's funny, I'm not afraid to talk to you now. I suppose it's because it's not going to make any difference. David will get what he wants from that book. But when I saw you in the Library it seemed so disloyal, not just talking to you about the outside, but—"

"Liking me?" Robert suggested.

Sophie nodded. They smiled shyly at each other, then Sophie said:

"And last night, I couldn't speak in front of David."

"You spoke out more than I did," Robert said.

"Yes, but I didn't *tell* you," Sophie said impatiently. "Why do you think I've always wanted to go to the land outside? It's not just curiosity. The Spell is like David; you can't think or feel independently while you're close to it, not without the most tremendous effort. And I had to try and think about something very strange."

Robert leaned forward in his chair, his eyes fixed on her face.

"When I was a little girl," Sophie continued, "my nurse took me out for a walk in the City. I don't think she was supposed to—she said it was a secret. We were going to visit her family in the western quarter, where the lantern makers and weavers have their shops. I was a naughty child, and I ran away. I found myself in an alley so far from the main street that the only noise came from my own feet on the cobbles. There was no one about. I was just beginning to get frightened, when I looked up at the wall of the house at the end of the alley—and I saw it."

"Saw what?"

"A carving up on the wall. It was very old and very dirty, but I knew it was the most important thing I had ever seen. It showed a young man with an ax standing under a tree."

"A picture of the true beginning," Robert breathed. "A picture of the Tree, here in the City!"

Sophie went on: "My nurse found me soon afterwards, scolded me half to death and took me home. It was years before I was allowed to go into the City by myself, and I never found that house again. Maybe it had been pulled down; it was very old and dilapidated. But I never forgot that carving. When I was older I learned about the Witch King and how he is to plant the Tree for the City. I knew the Tree must be linked to the tree I had seen. David told me that the prophesy meant reforming the Spell. I never quite believed him. But the carving was all I had, Robert! Not much to set against David's arguments. Not much to set against the Spell."

"But now you know the story from outside," Robert said. "Now you know that the Tree is the true beginning."

"If it is," Sophie said slowly, "what does that make the Spell?"

Before Robert could reply, the princess had jumped to her feet.

"I wish I had had the courage to talk to you earlier, or that we hadn't spoken about this at all," she said abruptly. "David has read that book now. Yesterday, when you agreed with him about the third prophesy, I was almost ready to accept being sent back, but now you say the Spell isn't the beginning who knows what I may find?"

"What?" Robert was on his feet too. "What are you talking about?"

She stared at him. "Didn't you realize? Of course that's stupid of me, only I'm so used to the idea. David is going to send me back to the beginning of the Spell to fetch it for him. He dares not risk going himself. If he's the Witch King he mustn't lose his triumph." She grimaced. "He's brought me up to be obedient. It's only one thing more."

Robert stared at her speechless and aghast.

"He *can't*," he said at last. He was already moving toward the door.

"But what are you going to do?" Sophie demanded, watching him with alarm.

"Stop him!" Robert said wildly, as he dragged open the door. Sophie called after him, but he was already running down the passageway toward the wizard's room without any notion of what he should do when he got there.

THIRTEEN

The door of Godfrey's study was half open when Robert reached it, and the quivering shadows betrayed the presence of a candle.

"Prince David!" The boy flung the door wide, but it was not the prince that he found. Godfrey's hawk face turned from the lectern toward his.

"A curious mistake," he murmured, folding his arms. "What should the prince be doing here?"

Robert's heart began to pound, and the blood drained from his face.

"He—I—" He got no further, and swallowed hard.

"This room was open when I reached it," the wizard said icily. "A book lies on the lectern that was in its place before supper. Who has been reading it?"

"The prince," Robert muttered with his eyes on his unpolished boots. He wished the earth would open and swallow him up.

"You let the prince into my study and left him to read that book? I see. Is that how you carry out my orders? And did the prince tell you what was in the book, Robert?"

Robert lifted his eyes, wincing as he met the wizard's cold green stare.

"He told me—" he began unsteadily, "he told me he was the Witch King, Godfrey. And I believed him last night, and even now I'm not sure he isn't. But he's going to send Sophie back to the beginning of the Spell. That isn't right, that's cowardly, whatever you think the Spell might be! And last night I was almost sure that the Spell was the beginning and David was right about how to mend it. Only the king said—" The wizard raised his hand impatiently.

"I've heard enough." The look of contempt on his face seemed to scorch Robert's heart.

"I knew you were a fool," Godfrey said. "But I didn't think David was quite a fool. Come here, boy, and see the trouble you have made between you."

Robert was unable to take even one step toward the lectern, but he found Godfrey's hand seizing him by the shoulder and pulling him close. The wizard kept that hand heavily in place on the base of Robert's neck, while with the other he opened the book and began to turn its pages.

"The man who wrote this went mad before he died," said the wizard. "At the end, you see, it trails off into babble and accusation. But he may have discovered something about the Spell others did not know, though he did not live to make his great experiment. Here—" he began to read in harsh jangling syllables that hurt Robert's ears.

"That," he explained, jabbing a sharp finger at the page, "describes what may be gained by the man who does not die or lose his wits somewhere along the passage back to the beginning. He gets mastery, this book claims. What the seven wizards spoke between them, he possesses in himself. The Spell enters him. He can control the kingdom, not like a king, but as a man controls his own body. More than that; our minds and hearts become his fingers' ends, to probe and feel at his will, to send obedient messages to his commanding brain." He paused and laughed harshly. "So the book claims. I suppose it is one way of fulfilling the prophesy, to save the City by destroying it."

Robert could hear no more. He twisted out of the wizard's grasp and turned to face him.

"What are we going to do?" he demanded urgently. "It's the princess he's going to send." He remembered her tears, and shook his head in despair. "She'll obey him. I don't understand how she can—"

"You obeyed him," the wizard said. "And when he was my pupil I—thought well of him." His green eyes grew hard and bright. "I thought he might be the one who is prophesied. It may be that he is. But if he chooses this way to fulfil the prophesies then the Witch King will have come to destroy the City merely to enlarge himself."

"We can stop him!" Robert exclaimed. "Let's go to the king."

Godfrey laughed. It was a thin, desolate sound like a pebble falling on ice.

"The king," he said, "can no longer help us. When I went to see him this evening, I found him unconscious. He is sleeping still. I doubt if he will ever wake."

"But he *can't* be so ill," said Robert. "When I saw him this morning—"

"That was before his grandson visited."

Robert turned white. "You mean David—" he could not bring himself to say it. "You mean that's why the king didn't prevent him from coming this evening?"

"The physicians can see nothing," Godfrey said. "But I believe I found some evidence of interference. Only David, besides myself, has that kind of skill. It comes down to my word against his, and I know whose word the nobles would trust. The order of regency is already before the council. By midnight David will be in command of the City."

"We must be able to do something," Robert persisted, "I can't let Sophie—"

"She must take her chance with the rest of us. Go to bed, boy, now—no arguing! I have to think. Perhaps David will listen to reason. If not—" Godfrey glanced back to the lectern and shook his head.

As Robert walked slowly toward the door the wizard was already reaching toward his books.

Robert lay awake most of that night. He tossed under his blankets till the sheets got twisted and his pillow was all in lumps. About two o'clock he got out of bed and went across to the window, opened it and leaned out. The kitchen yard beneath lay in deep shadow, rustling with cats. Beyond the yard was the dim shape of the west wing of the palace. Beyond that, in the darkness, lay the City.

"Why did I come here?" Robert asked aloud. "I've made such a mess of things."

The City gave no answer. Robert returned to his bed and lay down, feeling utterly alone. Toward dawn, as the birds began their noise, he fell asleep.

Almost at once, it seemed, he woke again. There was a
heavy weight pressing down on the bed by his feet. There
was a smell of tobacco. Robert sat up and rubbed his forehead in astonishment.

"Granny Fishbone. Hello," he said.

The moon, which was almost full, shone in through the
window suddenly as a cloud moved and lit up he cross old face.

"You're making a terrible mess of this business," she said.
"I can see it's time I took a hand. Where's that keepsake I
gave you? Lost it, I suppose, like you've lost your wits."

Robert tugged out the chain indignantly.

"You needn't make such a fuss," he said. "Of course I've
still got it. I even remember what you said. 'This came from
the City and now it must be returned.' "

"Bah! A schoolmaster's parrot can recite a lesson. What
does it *mean*, donkey?"

"I don't know." Robert sat up again and looked at the
keepsake in his hand. "There's nothing so very special about
it. It's just a fish made out of silver with a little fin on its
back and—oh!"

For as he touched the fin he released a secret spring; the
mouth of the fish opened, and something fell into his hand.

"What's this?" He stared at it. It lay in his palm, round,
tiny and hard, like a sea-smoothed bead.

"Granny Fishbone!" He looked up at her, eyes shining.
"It's the seed, isn't it? The seed from the Tree?"

She nodded, unsmiling. "And you are the bearer of it."

Robert stared at her. "But do you mean that *I'm*—"

"You are the Witch King, Robert," she said. "You must
save the City. You must plant the seed."

"I can't be the Witch King!" Robert cried. "I can't be. I just helped David find out all he needed about the Spell to destroy the City. How can I fight *him*? The Witch King must be someone else."

"Have you forgotten your dreams about the City?" Granny Fishbone said softly. "The blood of the Witch Women is strong in your veins, Robert. Your great-grandmother was a Witch Woman. That's why your grandmother believed the stories and your mother agreed to let you go. She can't quite believe in the City but she hopes for it. And you never thought of anything else since you first heard the stories."

"It's true."

Robert remembered his conviction that he would see the story of the Witch King come true and he smiled. A new confidence entered him. He stared down at the seed, so small and precious.

"Where did you get it?" he asked.

"It's been in my family a long time," Granny Fishbone said. "A wise king who knew we were good at keeping things sent it to us. Put it back, now, and close the mouth carefully. Carefully, I said! I have a little help to give you, Robert. The Spell is a powerful lie and it's eaten into the City. But there are older and more powerful things. One of them is the mosaic in the Sea Chamber. Do you remember what I told you about that?"

"You said it would come into its own when the Witch King came," Robert replied.

"Well, now he has come, and I am going to teach you the Spell that wakens its power," said Granny Fishbone.

"That's how it was in the old days, something from the kingdom bound up with something from the Witch Women. I am going to teach you how to summon the sea."

With her pipe in her mouth and her sleeves thrust up above her elbows, Granny Fishbone showed Robert the spell and got him to repeat it.

> "Restless waters, moon-swayed waters,
> By the moon's crooked finger I beckon you,
> Through the bright sea stones I summon you . . ."

When Robert reached the end she gave a grunt of satisfaction:

"You've got it. Good."

"How will I know when to use it?" asked Robert.

"You'll know," said Granny Fishbone. She twitched at her petticoats as though searching for her handkerchief. Robert turned his head politely. When he glanced back she was gone.

"Now that *is* strange," he said aloud. Could he smell tobacco after all? He was sitting up in bed, so it couldn't have been a dream. But the moon was gone and the gray light of dawn filled the room, and when Robert pressed the fin of the little fish its mouth stayed firmly shut. He did not think of looking under the bed for tobacco ash until late the next morning, and when he ran upstairs to see, he found that the floor had already been swept. Robert let it go. He had other things to worry about. The king was dying. Who could prevent David from sending his sister back to the beginning of the Spell?

FOURTEEN

Early next evening Wolf stood with folded arms before the king's door. Half a dozen paces from his feet sat Robert cross-legged upon the floor. He was waiting for Godfrey to come out of the king's apartment. One hand was closed on the silver fish on the chain around his neck. His face was white and strained. After Godfrey came out they were going to see the prince. Robert had little hope that David would listen to them. If he did not, Robert had resolved to go to Sophie and urge her to flee.

"At least that way Sophie will be safe," he told himself. "And David will think twice if he has to take the risk himself."

A low whistle from Wolf recalled him to immediate things. The king's door was open and Godfrey was coming out. He and Robert walked together to the prince's apartments, and were admitted at once. David led them into his study. He swept scrolls and loose papers off two upright wooden chairs and shut the door. Then he invited his guests to sit, while he himself leaned back against his desk, fixing his intense blue stare upon the wizard.

"My dear Godfrey," he began with evident relish, "I believe I can guess why you have come. Robert has told you my plans, hasn't he? But it's too late for that to matter. I now have all the information I need to put the Spell to my own use. Since you can't take that knowledge from me, you've come to plead with me not to use it. Shall I see if I can anticipate your argument? First will come the appeal to family feeling: it isn't *nice* to send one's sister into danger. Next, the tug of old tradition: no one's ever acted like this before, so David mustn't."

He laughed harshly. "Not very impressive, is it? So let's get down to the truth. You and the king always dress up your actions with fine words and far-fetched motives, but they come down to one thing in the end. You want to retain power. I don't blame you. Power's the one thing that is real. But nor can you blame me for going after it. I want the Spell and I want the throne. That's what the Witch King must be, a wizard and a king. I can be both, Godfrey! And don't mumble to me about tradition. All you mean by tradition is your retaining control." He laughed again. "I don't blame you for not relishing the change. It's not a pleasant prospect for a wizard, is it, to lose all control?"

Godfrey had lowered his eyes during this tirade. Now he looked up briefly.

"Robert, I don't need you," he said. "The prince admits his actions openly; we have no need of a witness. Go and get on with your work."

Startled, Robert gazed at him. The wizard had not set him any work today. Was it possible that Godfrey was giving him the opportunity to go to Sophie? But the wizard's cold stare gave him no clue, and David was growing aware of his hesitation. Quickly Robert got to his feet and left the room. Once he had gone Godfrey smiled faintly.

"David, I shan't try to persuade you that your argument is wrong. Far from being willing to get the truth, you seem interested only in having your own views confirmed. Whatever I say, you will attribute it to my alleged desire for power. Instead, let me ask you a question. What makes you think you have understood the writings of that book?"

"Whoever possesses the complete Spell possesses complete power," David answered. "That should be clear enough to you."

"And who will come into possession of the complete Spell? Not you, David."

"Sophie will remain under my complete control. The book says—"

"The book!" Godfrey retorted with contempt. "The ramblings of a madman that have never been tested. Really, David!"

David flushed with rage. "Don't use that tone toward me," he said. "That's how you used to treat me when I was your pupil. I took the rough side of your tongue for five years. I learned, though, and not just out of your books. I learned how to be charming and how to bide my time. And whenever a chance came to further my interests, I took it!"

Godfrey got to his feet. "There is no point in prolonging this. You say you are the Witch King, David, but I see no proof of it."

As he reached the door a loud cry came from the princess's apartment.

FIFTEEN

———— •◦• ————

Darkness was falling as Robert ran down Firefly Street toward the western gate. The watchmen had just sounded the short trumpet call which signaled the gate's closure for the night. Robert stared up at their flickering torches and the dark blue sky behind them and realized he was trapped in the City until morning. He walked right up to the closed gate and struck at it despairingly with his fist. It was over twelve feet high, studded with nails and curling metal clasps that gleamed in the torchlight above his head. A watchman shouted down, "What's going on there?" But Robert stayed very still and the shadows covered him and after a minute or two the watchmen set out on a patrol of the walls.

Robert sat down with his back to the gate and his face toward the City. Tears began to trickle slowly out of his eyes; after a minute he was sobbing and gasping like a fish twisting on a line. It had all happened so quickly. Sophie was glad to go with him. She had just come back out of her bedroom when the door burst open and David's servant ran in. He had a sword, and he was shouting something about a kidnaping; it was several seconds before Robert realized

he was being attacked. As the man bore down he backed
away. Something glittered in the firelight; Robert snatched
up the sword with his left hand and, as the man lunged at
him, he skipped sideways, slashing wildly as the other's
weight continued to carry him forward. He heard a cry and
saw the man crumple. To Robert's horror, blood started to
seep through his shirt as he fell; and as Sophie stooped over
him he groaned and twisted in pain. He was still alive, but
Robert had no time to feel relieved. There were footsteps
approaching on the stairs. He held out his hand to Sophie.

"Quickly!" he shouted. "We have to go!"

But she shook her head, her eyes dark with shock.

"David always wins," she said wildly. "Run, Robert! Run
before he kills you!"

Robert turned and ran, blundering past the guard on the
stairs, out of the palace and dodging through the park until
his lungs burned and tore, and still he ran until he had
reached the gate and could run no more. Now as he sat in
the darkness he accused himself bitterly. Whatever happened, he should not have left Sophie.

The last household noises reached him from Firefly
Street: the sound of water being thrown from a back door
into a paved yard; the cry of an infant and it's mother's lulla-
by. Candles winked out. Darkness and silence settled. As
the stars came out thickly overhead Robert wiped his wet
face with his hand. His mind had grown quiet. There was
nothing, for the moment, that he could do. Wherever Sophie
was she would be guarded. And if David was searching for
him, he knew he would not escape. He had tried, and failed
horribly. Now something or someone else must direct him.

Robert began to sing softly to himself. They were old songs, children's songs from the village. As he sang he remembered the sweet-leafed Tree that might yet grow in the king's park.

As the moon rose there was a rustling near him. A large rat swerved out of the ditch that ran beside the City wall and leaped over his feet. Its back gleamed in the moonlight as it darted up the street. Another followed, and still another dived across his legs and was lost in the darkness. Then the flesh of Robert's outstretched hand shivered violently. He glanced down and shook his hand with a shout. A large many-legged insect had been crawling over him. As he cast around he saw more of them slowly proceeding up Firefly Street toward the heart of the City. From around Robert now came other noises, slight rustling or hissing sounds, the dry creak of insect shells, the smoother passage of slugs and blindworms. The moon climbing the sky turned the mass of slime trails a sticky silver. As Robert watched, the moon seemed to light up the whole City. The creeping things were spreading inward from all directions, and Robert knew they were drawn by the evil that was preparing in the king's palace.

The vision grew stranger. Moonlight shone now through the houses of Firefly Street and fell on the sleeping faces of the lantern makers. Some took on a strange loveliness and others whitened into skulls. Following the sticky trail inward, the moonlight lingered on the merchants' houses. In one high white bed Robert saw gold shine molten, burning through a box to the hand that nursed it, burning that hand to the bone. Moonlight reached the king's palace and paused. It sifted the chalk dust in the flour of the baker who snored in his chair as the loaves baked. It shone upon the rich cloth of missing tunics, hidden in the wardrobes of the servants' quarters. It lit the dust that settled upon the papers of the scholars and the ink that reddened in their books wherever vanity had replaced the search for truth.

Moonlight crept across the walls of the palace into the rooms of the nobility. Here everything faded under it. The rich hangings grew very thin. The gold tarnished. Some of the sleeping bodies grew dry and brittle under the moon, the skins of faces yellow and papery; others slept as though a better air had quickened their dreams. The king's dragon blazed gold as the moonlight pierced it. Robert cried out with wonder as he saw the king. Under the moon he had grown younger. He slept like a man in the height of his strength, dark-haired, dark-bearded, calm. Robert watched him joyfully until the moon drew his eyes away to the Sea Chamber. Here the trail ended. The door and the walls about the door were saturated with slime and the creatures clambered over one another in their effort to draw closer.

A cloud suddenly passed over the moon, and for a moment darkness pressed at Robert's eyes. When the light returned it was in the Sea Chamber. Sophie and David were standing opposite each other, he on the platform, she on the ground at the front of the hall. Her dress was stained with the blood of the wounded man, her hair hung loose about her face and she was staring downward. Robert could not see her expression. David's voice came to him faintly. He had papers spread out before him, he raised his voice and began to chant. The voice grew louder and harsher.

To Robert the syllables seemed to twist and tear, hurting his ears with their jaggedness; then David spoke faster and it was worse, the words fusing together cruelly, continuing without hope of an end. Sophie stiffened. Her head jerked up and she looked steadily at her brother. She was breathing to the rhythm of his words, breathing them in and out, her heart pumping them into her. Her lips began to move painfully; as if around a mouthful of broken glass she began to chant with him. They were reaching the beginning of the Spell; around and behind them others appeared. At Sophie's back was the pressure of many bodies. She saw, and Robert saw with her, seven old men surrounding David upon the platform, each with a silver wand and an open book. Then her brother's voice stopped and he disappeared. Other voices began, and where David had been was another man, his dark face deeply lined. A heavy crown sat upon his brow.

It was King Leo.

For a moment longer Robert saw Sophie chanting with the wizards, then they and King Leo were gone and her body fell to the ground.

David walked unconcernedly away, content to let some servant find his sister in the morning. And Robert suddenly found himself back at the western gate, the vision over, his eyes sore and his limbs stiff. The moon had gone. Though it was too early for dawn, a thick yellow light was spreading across the sky from the direction of the palace. A cock crowed. It began to rain heavily.

SIXTEEN

By the time Robert reached the palace, birds were singing uncertainly and the gate watchmen had roused themselves. Their trumpets sounded faintly from the four quarters of the City as Robert slipped inside the palace by a side door. His heart thumped painfully against his ribs, but the guards at the palace gate had not challenged him so he guessed David, for some reason of his own, had chosen not to have him arrested.

The passageway leading to the kitchen was empty and dark and the smell of burnt bread hung heavily in the air. Robert followed the passage around to the door into the white-paneled hall and crossed it quickly toward the Sea Chamber. But before he reached the door he heard voices. Two women servants had already found Sophie and were doing their best to rouse her.

After a moment Robert turned away. He could not afford to let David discover him here, not until he had a clearer idea of what to do. He began to climb the stairs, encountering no one until he reached the king's door. There he found Godfrey, stretched like a hound across the threshold. Robert

stooped and shook him gently by the shoulder, and the
wizard twisted up into a sitting position, blinking rapidly
and shading his eyes with his arm as though Robert had
shone a bright light in his face. Slowly he lowered his arm
and looked confusedly at the boy. A cold horror welled up
in Robert. The eyes staring out of the wizard's yellow face
scarcely seemed to see him.

"Godfrey," he whispered urgently, putting his own hand
into the wizard's, "it's Robert. What has happened to you?"

The wizard's face strained painfully as if he could hear
Robert's words at an infinite distance.

"The Spell," he said at last with a great effort. "I felt
David begin the sending. Since then only confusion. I
cannot—" He gripped Robert's wrist so tightly that he let
out a yell of pain.

"I was afraid of this," Godfrey continued, the words
spewing from him in spasms. "You must do what you can,
Robert. Perhaps, after all, an outsider—and there is no one
else."

His hand slipped away and he lay down again as if exhausted. Robert did not like to leave him alone but as the
minutes passed and the wizard did not stir he got up and
entered the king's apartment.

The first chamber was empty and cold; no fire had been
lit in the grate since the king had been found unconscious.
Robert opened the inner door. The room was gloomy, the
heavy curtains drawn. Robert made out an indistinct shape,
the king's bed and, in it, the king. Unwilling to open the
curtains and admit the strange yellow light, Robert took a
candle from the mantelpiece and lit it at the fire which

smouldered under the ash in the bedroom grate. Then he went over to the bed. The king stirred as he approached.

"What time is it?" he asked in a faint, cracked whisper.

"You're awake!" Robert exclaimed joyfully.

"Robert?" Slowly the king's head rose a little on the pillow and his old eyes, watery and blue, opened. "I have had strange dreams," he murmured, almost to himself. "And what news do you bring?"

Robert's hand holding the candle shook so that light spilled across the King's rich quilt.

"The prince has sent Sophie back to the beginning of the Spell," he said in a low voice. "I tried to help Sophie escape, but David sent a guard and I—I stabbed him."

The king sighed.

"Fetch me that bowl from the table there, Robert. And help me to raise my head. My body is weak and I must feed it a little or I will not be able to manage it at all."

Robert fetched the bowl and helped the king to sip a little of the milk it contained.

"You should have attendants," he scolded. "You could have—anything might have happened in the night."

The king smiled. "The crown is a terrible prize, Robert, and a great temptation to encourage a man's dying once you've got him to begin. But I am glad to have been left in peace."

He settled his head back upon the pillow. Then he continued in a stronger voice:

"So you have stabbed a man, Robert Harding. And David has sent Sophie into the Spell."

"I helped him," Robert said in a shaky voice. "I let him

see that book. If I had refused, the rest of it—Sophie, and that man—" He broke off, as the appalling cry and the blood rose again to confront him.

"Robert, my son, look at me." The strength and love and the conviction in the king's voice brought fresh tears to Robert's eyes as he slowly raised them to meet the old man's gaze.

"You must endure the thought that you cannot undo what is past. We all must. I have been tormented by the memory of David after his father's death. I was too busy with state affairs to see him. I slipped into the habit of relying on his tutors and governors for reports, which were, of course, always excellent. I loved him, but at such a distance of neglect! And now I realize that I hardly knew him at all."

The old man sighed and, reaching a hand under his pillow, produced a small packet. "This is for you." As Robert turned it over uncertainly in his hands the king added, "You are meant to open it."

Robert opened the packet. Into his hand spilled two rings. One he recognized at once. Smooth heavy gold, with the dragon's head stamped on it, it was the ring of kingship. He glanced up at the king in astonishment. The king nodded.

"I told you I have had strange dreams. I saw you walking by the sea with a Witch Woman. And I saw you stooping to plant a seed in the ground outside the palace. I believe your stories are the true ones, Robert. The City did exist before the Spell. And when you become king the seed and the Tree will renew it once again."

"But what about Prince David?" Robert asked. "He is your heir. I can't usurp his place."

The king was silent. Then he said:

"I do not know how this is to happen. But I know it must. If David succeeds, his kingship will bring horror and the triumph of the Spell. Your task may take years of suffering. It will require his death. But David is mortal and the Spell is a lie. You *will* win, Robert. The Witch King will succeed.

"I gave you another ring," the king continued. "Do you know what it is?"

Robert looked at it. It was slight and small, made of silver.

"I gave that ring to my own wife when we were married," the king said. "I promised it to Sophie for a wedding ring. I give you my blessing with it."

Robert bowed his head. A longing to see Sophie filled him, though a wedding ring to offer her seemed at that moment almost a mockery. But the king continued serenely:

"My great-grandchildren will visit the Witch Women. Your children, Robert, and Sophie's. I know you will find a way to rescue her. I know you will find a way to defeat the Spell."

As Robert stared at him in silent hope, the old man smiled. "You must go now, Robert, and wait for David's next move. Find a place where you can wait safely. I do not think he will try to use the Spell until he has made sure that I am dead."

"You think he might kill you?" Robert said, appalled. "Then I'm not going to leave you."

But the king shook his head.

"I am not certain of it. I do know that you must go, Robert, before there are too many people about."

Still Robert did not move. "I want to stay with you," he said.

The king smiled. "What for? I am not afraid of the dark. Go now. I insist on it."

Robert bent to kiss his frail hand and left.

SEVENTEEN

———— ◆ •• ◆ ————

By late afternoon a soft yellow fog began to chill the City to its carved bones. Cold and faint with hunger, Robert slipped out from his hiding place under the dais in the Sea Chamber and went to stand by the window.

He could see nothing beyond the glass. Beads of moisture ran down the wall beside him and through the doorway into the great hall he could see the hangings looking dull and faded, their silver and gold threads gleaming faintly as though the strange yellow air had tarnished them. A fire had been lit in the huge stone fireplace but its heat did not penetrate the Sea Chamber. Robert looked longingly toward its smoky light.

Coldness and heaviness grew on him as he waited. It was as if the air itself was growing thicker, its pressure building up in his lungs and brain, making it harder to think. He stared dully at the blank windows, not wanting to turn around anymore. He could feel the wall of the opposite side of the room right behind his back as if it were about to close on him and crush him, but when he turned to look, it appeared distant and frail as paper, as if a touch would tumble it. He knew it was David's magic affecting him as it had affected Godfrey so much more deeply; and he rubbed his eyes tiredly and tried not to allow his fear to grow. Just as he had decided to return to his hiding place, he heard a faint note of trumpets from deep inside the palace, followed by a shout. The noise was repeated, gradually growing louder and closer until Robert heard the words: "The king is dead. Long live the king!"

He stood quite still. Beneath the dullness induced by David's magic he felt a pain as sharp as a sword. But there was no time to mourn for the old king. David would act now and Robert had to be ready to oppose him.

Almost at once there was a noise outside the door and the first of the crowd began to arrive. Robert ran toward the dais and hid around the side of it. He saw Wolf take his stand at the corner of the platform, leaning against it sword in hand and screening Robert from view. The other servants followed, taking their places at the back of the hall. When the ladies of the court began to arrive it was clear no one knew quite what to expect. Some wore purple and black, the colors of mourning; others had dressed for the new king in white and gold. Dresses rustled and swept across the polished floor, perfumes mingled in the air, but there were no voices and no laughter. Children stood beside their mothers without fidgeting, their heavy eyes fixed on the empty dais. The lords took their places and still the silence was unbroken. Then the king's trumpets sounded the fanfare and the solemn procession began.

As it crossed the hall there was a ripple of ragged laughter. The king was magnificent, faintly smiling as he passed through the crowd in his coronation robes. But the two young pages who held the end of his train kept turning to stare behind them at the wizard. Godfrey seemed blind or crazed. His head turned wildly; seeing and yet not seeing, he danced and shied down the hall. Wherever he passed laughter began and fell away, silenced by the terror expressed in the wizard's face. Behind the wizard came a stretcher supported by two servants bearing the rigid body of the princess. The crowd murmured with pity and surprise; Sophie's eyes were open and staring.

The new king mounted the steps of the dais. His eyes swept over the crowd and he smiled a smile that was both hungry and complacent. He pointed to a space on the ground close to the platform and here the servants laid the stretcher, then stepped aside.

"My people!" the king cried. "My friends. You will think it strange that I should appear before you all clothed in the robes of my coronation when the dead king lies unburied upstairs. But I am no mere successor of the dead. I am the restorer and the renewer of first intentions. My people, the hour of the Witch King has come!" David's voice rang through the Sea Chamber like a trumpet. "This is the time of the prophesies' fulfilment. You will see the Spell blossom into fullness once more."

"No!" Robert's voice echoed through the Sea Chamber.

"No, David," he repeated, walking unopposed to the bottom of the steps. "That is not the way to fulfil the prophesies. Can't you see that the Spell is not the seed? It does not spring from the beginning."

He raised his voice so that the whole crowd could hear.

"How could this good City have sprung from that? Besides, the palace was already built! I saw the wizards here in the Sea Chamber saying the Spell for the first time with the City already built and active around them. How could that have been the beginning? Let the Spell go, David. Bring Sophie back."

No one in the crowd stirred or responded. Their eyes were fixed on David, who smiled dangerously.

"Wolf!" he called. "Remove this babbler."

Out of the corner of his eye Robert saw Wolf approaching. He climbed up the steps to where David stood.

"Here!" he shouted, pulling out the silver fish that hung around his neck and holding it up for all to see. "The seed of the prophesies is here, the seed that was kept and hidden for future need when the first Tree fell. It is mine, David. I will take it and plant it as the prophesy says!"

For a moment David's smile wavered. Then he shook his head incredulously and smiled again, as at a child's fantasy. Robert felt Wolf's hand grasp his ankle and he was jerked to the ground.

Robert struggled frantically, and shouted at Wolf:

"Don't you understand? He is going to destroy Sophie!" But his voice was drowned by the great cry with which David raised his arms to begin his magic. He spoke the familiar Word of Entry, but his voice made it twist harshly in his listeners' ears. At the first syllable Robert saw Godfrey stiffen and his agitation cease. Wolf loosened his grip upon Robert and upon his sword. When the latter slipped out of his hands and crashed to the floor no one heeded it. All eyes were fixed upon David. Another face was moving upon his as though the two were growing together, fusing into one. As Robert watched he remembered the confused images of the Spell and himself among them, up on the dais. What he had seen in the Spell on his first evening in the City was happening now. The face became stronger, clearer, blotting out David's face. As David's voice began to fade, Robert gave a groan of recognition. He was in the presence of King Leo and the wizards.

EIGHTEEN

K ing Leo turned to the old men who flanked him to the
left and to the right. At his signal they opened the books
they carried. Then he turned back to the assembly. His
broad face was bearded with soft dark hair, his eyes glittered
with a cold pride. There was something terrible in the delib-
eration of his movements. He spoke a word of command,
and like a wind shivering through trees, the same expression
of fear and horror crossed the faces of the old men. As the
first grating syllables of the chant began, a shrill protesting
scream cut across it. Startled, Robert turned. Close to the
front, among others dressed in the strange fashion of another
age, stood a woman in a plain white linen robe. Her hair
was shaken down around her face and her head moved
wildly in her struggle to free herself from the grip of two
liveried men. It was her mouth that had screamed and now
it screamed again.

"The children, Leo! What have you done with the
children?"

No one in the hall turned to answer her.

"Judith," Robert whispered. He stretched out his hand

toward her as though to comfort her. At that moment he saw Sophie rise.

She moved to stand at Judith's side, her eyes fixed upon Leo, her mouth moving to the rhythm of the chant. The wizards' voices were gradually rising, the noise becoming harsher and less endurable as the end approached. Fierce pain forced Robert's hands over his ears. He saw an agony in the faces around him, tears of rage in the king's eyes. The guards let go of their prisoner and dropped to the ground, burying their heads in their arms.

Mad Judith stood exultant. The pain caused by the making of the Spell delighted her. She found some recompense for her own unbearable loss in seeing others suffer. As the last word crashed against Robert's heart, he saw Sophie turn and cling to her. For a moment Sophie and Judith were united in an embrace and then, when silence fell, Judith was gone. The vision was over and the scene had returned to normal.

As Robert scrambled to his feet, shaking the pain out of his head, he heard quiet laughter. Godfrey was standing upright on the dais, looking about him as if he were seeing the place for the first time. His green eyes reached Robert and a slow smile broke across his thin face.

"You are right about the City," he called down. "It *is* older than the Spell. And now the Spell has left me. I am free of it. We are all free of it!"

Around the room men and women were still lying on the ground or bent double in the positions of pain into which the vision had thrown them. But it was true, Robert realized. They were free, and he knew why. The Spell had entered

Sophie, as the book had predicted. The words that were only a vague and terrible memory to the others were concentrated in her mind and heart.

David began to descend the steps to her.

She stood with her eyes shut, one hand beating lightly against her side to the rhythm of the Spell, her head slightly cocked as though she were listening. No one else could hear the Spell any more but Sophie's lips continued to repeat the first terrible words in silence. Across the hall men and women in the act of comforting one another stopped and watched as David spoke to his sister.

"Sophie," he said gently, "do you know where you are? Do you know who I am?"

She nodded, her lips still moving. Her head began to turn, blindly searching the room for a means of escape.

"You are—the king," she said. Suddenly another voice, not Sophie's, forced its way out of her throat.

"Leo, where are the children?" Her mouth opened wider and a deep wailing issued from it. Then her lips returned to their silent chanting.

David put his hand forward and touched her cheek. She did not respond. He grasped her arm and pulled her toward him, half-turning to the wizard.

"What is the matter with her?" His voice rose in panic. "I can't get her to respond to me. The Spell is in there, but so is something else."

"Ask the Witch King," said Godfrey quietly, descending the steps. "He has the clearest eyes."

David turned around and glared at Robert.

"Do you mean *him*?" he shouted, then pushed his sister toward Godfrey. "No! You do it, wizard! And do not speak of an outsider ruling *my* kingdom."

Godfrey caught Sophie by the shoulders and held her gently.

"Tell me how to get rid of the—the thing in her." David gestured with a violent hand. "Make her open up to me."

"I cannot," Godfrey said. He called to Robert. "Will you explain to us what has happened?"

Robert came forward slowly, his eyes fixed on Sophie.

"When the princess returned she brought Judith with her," he said in a voice that shook. "Sophie is clinging to her. I do not know what Judith wants. The Spell, perhaps, or revenge for her dead children."

There was a pause. Then David addressed Godfrey as if it was he who had spoken.

"How can I get rid of Judith?"

"Only by helping Sophie cast her off," Robert said. "Only by letting Sophie abandon the Spell."

David pushed him away and shouted at Godfrey:

"Wizard, you will make Sophie surrender the Spell to me!"

Godfrey shook his head. "I will not."

"Wolf!" David roared across the hall. "Fetch me your sword."

Like a sleepwalker Wolf rose from his corner and stumbled toward the king. He had understood nothing of what had happened. The pain of losing the Spell had shattered his mind. He had forgotten why he had been carrying a sword, but he heard a familiar voice of command, saw the weapon on the ground and obeyed.

Robert seized his arm as he approached, but Wolf shook him off, striking him across the face with such strength that Robert was knocked to the ground. Then he presented the hilt of the sword to David, who took it and stepped toward Godfrey. The wizard gently put Sophie to one side of him and stood with his eyes fixed steadily on the king's face.

"Godfrey," said David almost in a whisper, "I will kill you if you don't obey."

"David." Godfrey's thin face relaxed into a smile that made the king peer forward in bewilderment. "If I wanted to do the thing you tell me, I could not. You have locked up the Spell in Sophie, don't you see? You have left me powerless."

David's hand tightened on his sword. Sweat pricked his face. He licked his lips.

"I don't believe you," he said.

Godfrey's eyes, meeting his, grew stern. "I am speaking the truth."

With a shout of rage David rushed at him. He ran his sword through the wizard's body. Godfrey fell forward gasping, his arms extended almost as if to embrace him. David stepped back, tugging his sword free. As Robert ran forward with a cry of horror, Godfrey's body crumpled to the floor. David turned and faced the people, brandishing the wet sword.

"So perish all who challenge the Spell or my right to it." But his sword arm trembled so violently that he had to lower it again.

"Now Sophie or Judith or whoever you are," he said, "you must give me the Spell."

"Don't make her say it!" Robert cried from where he was kneeling at the side of the dead wizard.

"Look, I'll say it with you," David continued. "I'll start the Word of Entry and then you can take over." At once he began, catching Sophie's wrists and driving the words into her with all the force he could summon.

As Robert got to his feet he heard Judith's voice begin to chant in Sophie's mouth. Sophie's eyelids fluttered and opened, showing blue eyes, Judith's eyes. The voice grew stronger and David ceased to chant, though his lips continued to move silently. A strange yellow fog began to play over Sophie's face. It began to blur and change until it was no longer Sophie's face but Judith's. Judith's fingers stretched out and, with a quick motion, it was she who was holding David's wrists. David grew faint and ghost-like as Judith drained his spirit and his soul. He fell to the ground, dead, and Judith turned toward the crowd.

She swept through them chanting the Spell and where she passed the people withered like grass and fell. Those who remained stood motionless, held by her will. She reached the windows, still chanting and breathed into the fog, turning it a dark burning red. The City and its people were hers. Only Robert was left free.

"You have something I want," Judith said. "Give it to me."

Robert closed his hand on the fish about his neck.

"The seed belongs to the City, Witch King, and the City is mine."

Robert shook his head. "Search the Spell," he said. "Among everything you have taken is there the peace you are seeking?"

She shook her head slowly and moaned till the hall echoed. "My children are not there."

"Then why take the seed?" asked Robert. "It will not take their place."

She started toward him.

"It might bring me peace to eat the seed. It might fill their place. Everything would be mine then and I would sleep."

"No!" Robert shouted. "If you want peace, Judith, you must leave the Spell and go back to your place. You can let it go. And you *must* let Sophie go. If you swallow the seed, I tell you the Tree will burst out of your flesh and grow up through it. It cannot be trapped inside the Spell."

Judith made no answer. She came forward steadily, eyes fixed upon his neck. Robert backed away, but Judith whipped out a hand and, before he could react, she had snapped the chain off his neck. He could only watch her fingers stroke and squeeze, searching the fish for an entrance, seeking the hidden spring. Then, noiselessly, the mouth of the fish slid open and the seed rested in the palm of Judith's hand.

"*Sophie!*" Robert shouted desperately. "Make her go, fight her!"

There was no response. Robert's eyes swept past her and fell upon the chaos of the mosaic, the green and black and violet of the sea. He remembered the spell Granny Fishbone had taught him.

"But I can't summon the sea," he thought. "If I do, what will happen to Sophie?" Then Judith's hand began to move slowly up to her mouth. Robert cried out:

"Sophie, forgive me!" and, trusting to Granny Fishbone, began to chant.

> "Restless waters, moon-swayed waters,
> By the moon's crooked finger I beckon you,
> Through the bright sea stones I summon you . . ."

At the first word, Judith raised her head sharply. Her eyes glared and her hand paused.

"What is it?" she hissed.

Robert continued, reciting faster.

Judith became frantic. Her head began to turn violently. As Robert reached the end her mouth opened in a strangled cry, through which Sophie's voice suddenly emerged.

"Robert. Help me!"

He stretched forward one hand. "Sophie?" he whispered.

"Help me, I can't—"

Her voice was lost in the noise of Judith's angry wail. Then, on the wall behind them, a corner of the mosaic began to spin and dissolve and spurt out water. It was an area no bigger than a coin but the mosaic seemed to melt around it and the trickle grew. Green and foaming sea-water spilled out of the wall onto the floor and swept across it. Judith turned in alarm. Her face contracted in terror and she gave a howl of despair.

"Yes!" cried Sophie's voice exultantly. Judith's arm jerked

and her hand dropped open, abandoning the seed and its metal case.

Robert stooped to snatch up the precious things. As he rose it was Sophie he saw, her face alight with triumph. Before he could move toward her he was knocked off his feet by a crashing roar. Wet salt darkness overtook him. The sea had returned to the City.

NINETEEN

Robert was thrown upward by the force of water and then plunged backward through confusion and darkness, the sea waves sucking him down head first, his back arching painfully and his arms pressed to his side. He fought his urgent need to draw breath, though the burning pain in his lungs and the black pressure inside his head threatened to force him. Just as his mouth opened to inhale the sea, his feet struck the floor, the water fell away from him like a suffocating cloak and he drew a long shuddering breath of cool air. Light danced on his eyelids.

When he could bear to open them his eyes told him he was still in the Sea Chamber. At least the room was the right size and shape—everything else was changed. The windows were smashed and the dais broken. Strangest of all, the mosaic had gone. Only pock-marked plaster remained on walls that stank of salt and oozed moisture. Around him men and women, freed from Judith's power, were struggling to their feet. An incredulous joy began to register on their faces. Judith was gone and they were alive! And Robert, searching the faces of the crowd, shared that joy. Sophie was standing by the dais, with her head on one side and her wet hair swinging across her cheek. She was shaking the water out of her ears as though she had just been swimming.

Robert immediately took charge. He sent Wolf down to the City to bring back a report of the flood damage, and got the other servants to carry out the injured and the dead. The women set about providing hot food and dry clothes, while the men began the long task of clearing away the wreckage. But when the heralds asked whom they should proclaim King David's successor, Robert told them to wait. He went instead to Sophie and asked her to come out with him into the park.

There was a ridge of high ground that had escaped the downward rush of the salt tide and rose like a green island from the waste of rank mud. They went to it and stood together looking down at the City in the evening light.

"What happened to you?" Robert asked. "Do you remember any of it?"

"It's difficult to describe," Sophie said. "I felt as though I was asleep. It was like being held in someone's arms. I heard David's voice and then yours, but so faintly, and all the time Judith was—singing lullabies, you might say. Then you shouted something. It hurt, like being pricked or pinched. It went on pinching, insisting that I wake up and then I realized that what you were saying came from outside." She bit her lip. "I'd forgotten there *was* anything outside. When the guard attacked you and I realized David planned to have you killed, I panicked. David seemed too powerful to resist.

I just gave up. But I had to get away from the Spell. That's why I turned to Judith and let her take over. When I heard you, I knew I could fight back. I felt what was in her— my—hand, and I forced her to give it up." She smiled, but her smile shook.

"So Judith's ghost was swept away with the Spell when all she really wanted was her children."

Robert shook his head.

"She wanted to destroy us all. You can't feel sorry for her!"

Sophie said nothing. She turned and looked over her shoulder at the palace. Seeing only the fine curve of her neck and jaw and the heavy beauty of her hair, Robert could not guess what she was thinking. His hand closed on the two rings in his pocket and he cleared his throat nervously. Then Sophie said:

"If I had come with you then, if I had resisted David, none of this might have happened." She began to cry silently, and he forgot his own feelings in the need to comfort her. He took her hand.

"I don't think any of us are as important as that," he said. Startled, she looked up at him. "All of us made it happen. If you and I had been less timid, or the old king had been less busy, or Godfrey had been less certain, perhaps between us we might have avoided this. But I don't quite know how. Remember how old the Spell was, old and heavy with the weight of all the kings and the people that lived under it. When things are allowed to get very bad, it costs a lot to put them right." He hesitated, then added, "Part of the price is knowing you've made some mistakes."

Sophie stared at him. "But you've nothing to regret," she said. "You saved us."

Robert looked down at the City. The sun had set. The sky was darkening to the east and the air was growing cold.

"I left you," he said stubbornly. "I left you to—all that."

Sophie laughed. It was an odd, hiccuping laugh because she was still so close to tears.

"But I told you to go. I wanted you to escape. It was wrong, I know. But I thought David was bound to win. I thought if I gave him what he wanted, at least he might let you go."

Robert hardly dared meet her eyes. But he began to hope a little.

He felt inside his shirt for the silver fish and pulled the chain off over his head. He pressed the secret catch and the seed slipped into his hand. He looked at Sophie and drew a large breath.

"I wouldn't have this now if it wasn't for you," he said "Shall I plant it here?"

Sophie nodded.

Robert took out his knife. With one hand he unclasped it and drilled a hole in the turf. He dropped the seed into the rich black earth and covered it over, then slowly stood up, brushing his hands on his trousers. It was such a small thing to have done, so ordinary, that he felt a stab of disappointment. But Sophie's eyes were shining. "It'll grow in secret," she said. "The City will wake one day to the scent of the leaves."

"And everything will begin again," said Robert.

"Sophie," he said in a changed voice, "when the worst of the clearing up is over and we have a little time, I'd like to go home and see my family. Will you come?"

"To the outside?" Delight lit up her face. "With you? Not with a royal escort of three hundred horsemen?"

He grinned to see she remembered their old joke.

"A royal princess will be quite enough," he said. "My mother will have to get out her best tablecloth."

He reached into his pocket and pulled out the two rings.

"The old king gave me these. He meant that the two should go together, but of course I don't expect—" He swallowed and went on quickly. "You are so smart and so beautiful you could have anyone you like. But I'm going to ask you anyway. Will you marry me, Sophie?"

Sophie smiled at him and touched his hand.

"Of course I will," she said.

He slipped the silver ring onto her finger and then the gold ring onto his own.

"Now they can proclaim it," he said, and kissed her. "Now they can proclaim me king."

Granny Fishbone was down on the beach beyond the village, poking among the seaweed and spars at the water's edge, when a glittering on the hillside caught her eye. She got to her feet and frowned. A green and gold banner flashed again in the sunlight as a horseman rode slowly down the hill. Two heralds followed him on foot. They halted outside the village and the fanfare of their trumpets reached Granny Fishbone faintly. Children ran into the street, shouting to their parents to come and see. As the villagers crowded out of doors, a king on a white horse, with his queen beside him, rode down into the village.

Granny Fishbone dropped her stick.

"So the boy came home," she said. And she set off across the sand toward him.